Blood Brothers, Soul Sisters

TERRY PRONE

POOLBEG

Published in 1994 by
Poolbeg,
A division of Poolbeg Enterprises Ltd,
Knocksedan House,
123 Baldoyle Industrial Estate,
Dublin 13, Ireland

A catalogue record for this book is available from the British Library.

ISBN 1 85371 402 X

Cover drawing *Out of the Head* by Brian Bourke
Cover design by Poolbeg Group Services Ltd/Red Dog Graphics
Set by Poolbeg Group Services Ltd in Garamond 10/13
Printed by The Guernsey Press Company Ltd,
Vale, Guernsey, Channel Islands.

For the maestro,
In mannered subservience

Author's Note

Some of these stories have not previously appeared in print.

The Dependants and *The Intervention* were published by David Marcus in his 'New Irish Writing' in the *Irish Press*. Both were presented under a pseudonym.

A slightly different version of *The Scattering of Mrs Blake* appeared in *The Scattering of Mrs Blake and Related Matters*, published by Marion Boyars, London, 1987.

A section of *Blood Brothers, Soul Sisters* first appeared in a playlet commissioned by the Vincent de Paul Society.

Wheezy Weather was first published in the *Irish Medical Times*.

Contents

BLOOD BROTHERS, SOUL SISTERS

ONE AFTERNOON, HE DECIDED TO GO HOME.

He tried the sentence out for size.

"One afternoon, he decided to go home."

But it was not quite true, he reflected. The sentence sounded as if he were in charge of his life. It suggested the tough decisiveness of a body-builder bench-pressing three hundred pounds, face varicosed in the agony so visually reminiscent of orgasm.

He tried that phrase out too. "Visually reminiscent of orgasm."

He could not pinpoint when he had begun this commentary on his life as he lived it, articulated in his head but unspoken. In the morning when the alarm clock gave its throat-clearing noise preparatory to ringing: he would lie on his back in bed and the commentary would start up. It was a way of observing his life and yet distancing him from it, so that he frequently had to pull his concentration back to reality, the way you pull your eyes back into focus when tiredness has diluted the precision of your gaze.

In theory, his commentary acknowledged, it was undoubtedly he who had made the decision to go home.

In practice, the decision had possessed him. Not as a demon. More as a car is possessed on foot of non-payment. One afternoon a decision had made him . . .

But then, the earlier decision had made him, too. The decision to leave the flat in Rathmines and go to London. For a year. Or two.

"It may be for years and it may be forever," his father warbled at the time, to distract his mother. Clemmie Hogan was like a natural steam eruption. Her emotional pressure built up, usually over a period of an hour, and resulted in regular ear-splitting explosions of hysteria.

Her husband had learned, early in the relationship, that a well-timed laugh could abort the purgative cycle, and had subsequently worked to make himself a master of the one-liner. The two of them were definitively happy, although most people outside the family found Paul Hogan's rapid-fire jollities as wearing as long-term hiccups.

It had not been for years. It had been for eighteen months. In Chelsea. In a group of pre-War apartments overlooking a garden so darkened by the tall surrounding buildings that it looked like the bottom of an ill-lit aquarium, dark green spiky foliage ever-present, yet never growing further from the darker soil. On the second floor of the apartments was an excellent restaurant visited by the inhabitants.

"Relics of oul' dacency," his father had said, on his lone visit, looking around at the cardiganed and bent old men and women, closer to Rattigan characters than to life.

They had liked him, the genteel old inhabitants. They had liked him because he was soft-spoken. Courteous. And unhurried.

That was happening to him more and more, he noted. Even his thoughts were breaking into staccato phrases, in time with his breathing.

This is a long, long corridor, his internal commentator observed. Why? Concentrate, now.

Oh, yes. On the other side is the duty free, the brown bottles of Bailey's and the twinned white and black of Sheridans and the sillier tourist trap tripe-drinks all competing in two prices for favour/favor.

He paused to look out of the window, letting the other passengers pass him by. Small commuter planes on the parking area. Shortts? Perhaps Fokkers. From somewhere in the ill-sorted files of his memory surged the open-pored fat face of a TV comedian.

"So this war hero is telling the story of how he was shot right out of the sky, and he's telling the interviewer, 'these fokkers came from nowhere, three of them, and dey go bang bang and I lose de ving, and I know I go down – ' and the interviewer says to the camera, 'I suppose I should make it clear that Fokker is the name of a wartime plane', and the war hero says 'No, no, you don't understand. Dese fokkers were Messerschmidts!'"

When he had first heard it, he had been a teenager in a home where bad language was not approved of and he remembered the exhilaration of telling it to his parents, knowing that the laughter it provoked would allow him to get away with the 'dirty words'. Smiling at the memory, he resumed his walk down the long corridor. A group of sleek young executives beamed knowingly at him from an IDA poster at the end of the corridor. They were young, those IDA faces. Young. Glowing. Eyes unaccustomed to fear or compromise. He hated them.

No, he amended, as the moving staircase took him down to the baggage retrieval area, he didn't hate them. His reaction to them was the same reaction Irish people have when visiting France the first time. Aren't the children clever. To speak French so well. Aren't the IDA kids annoying. To have such notions of immortality. Or worse.

To have no need for notions of mortality or immortality.

The customs officer ignored him as he pushed the trolley carrying his two old cases through the blue channel. The grey glass doors opened as he approached, and he turned the wheels to bring him into the fenced-off square outside which the welcomers were supposed to sit. As always, children had invaded the square and arrivers with trolleys full of luggage were blocking the two exit areas. He stood, momentarily, his eye caught by an airport feature new since his last visit; angular miniature rostrums. Lit up from inside. Red, white and blue. Five of them. Poles linked them to the ceiling and a foot above head level a dotted red electronic sign, always moving to the left, said Welcome to Dublin in high-tech repetitious parody of the clutchers and kissers around him.

His sister nodded and rolled her eyes up to heaven at the new arrivals who were preventing the two of them from meeting. When the traffic unjammed, she surged at him, her unmade-up face soft and cold against his cheek. She hugged him long and hard. Eventually, he gently disengaged from her.

"Think you'd hold on a bit longer," she muttered cheerfully. "Best-looking man in the airport giving me a hug. Some of us are not that well endowed with gorgeous hunks, you know."

"Probably compensation."

"Mmmm?" She was feeding her parking card into the machine. Neatly, he thought. Neatly and surely. She would have the right change, he knew. She did. And would want a receipt.

She did.

"For being well-endowed elsewhere," he finished. She gave the quick token laugh she always did. A laugh that said. "Not funny. But we'll go along with it." A habit of preoccupied motherhood.

She stumped ahead of him, her every footfall self-assured and overt, as if making a point.

The hatchback swung up and he hoisted the luggage into the boot. Ramps everywhere these days for invalids. Oops – for People with Disabilities. He wondered about the freedom of the disability badge, the stick figure with the wheelchair wheel. The freedom not to have to pretend to be well and strong and vigorous. The freedom of childhood, when an adult hand pulls the curtains against the noisy brightness of the day and tucks the bedclothes firmly in around the fever. When there is permission to let go and sink softly into the sweaty half-comfort of midday dozing.

Marion drove badly, as she always had. She never seemed capable of seeing further away than ten yards, so when other cars braked or when traffic lights turned red, it came as a surprise to be coped with, rather than a logical inevitability. His luggage shifted in the boot and he wondered if he had padded the oversized framed Mapplethorpe sufficiently. On the other hand, his internal commentator observed, there would be a certain circular aptness to arriving home on this occasion with a framed Mapplethorpe half-visible behind shattered glass.

" . . . so I've just given up. You can do so much, and then you have to let whatever happens, happen."

His sister was in full flow, he realised, and he had missed what the subject was. But the questions to cover his failure to listen came with the custom of years.

"Not an easy lesson?"

"No. But there comes a time. Thanks for the signal, buddy."

This to a Fiat which had cut in ahead of her. Feargal had been watching the Fiat for some time. Its driver had been indicating his intent clearly for at least a minute and a half.

"Derek is living with some bright girl in Dublin and she's going to leave him in due course, because she's doing very well and she'll get a scholarship and go off to Moscow or somewhere. She studies Russian."

The car surged out onto the N4 and Feargal consciously relaxed his legs, willing himself not to push against non-existent brakes on his side of the vehicle.

"And Pádraig?"

"Pádraig is still at home. Applying to all the RTCs, now it's clear he'll never get into a university. He doesn't have his uncle's capacity for getting his head down and studying."

Feargal smiled.

"His uncle probably studied hard for the wrong reasons."

She looked at him sideways and he fought down the desire to tell her to watch the road ahead.

"I think I studied because I had nothing else to do. I never really fitted in at UCD. I wasn't a great sportsman and I wasn't a debater and I hated most of the social life. So what else was there to do?"

"Yeah, well I wish my pair had less interest in sport and social life. Derek had the bloody nerve to say to me recently that I was being rigid and that what he wanted to be was a Renaissance man."

Feargal laughed until a bout of coughing stopped him. Marion turned off the heater in the car as if it was to blame.

"A Renaissance man!"

She suddenly pulled out to pass an articulated lorry and Feargal's internal commentator began to pray, in the language of his childhood. Oh Jesus Mary and Joseph, save me in this hour of danger and I will never, ever, as long as I live, I swear to God, ever again – The lorry was successfully passed and Feargal pondered the realisation that he had run out of bribes for God. This must be some rite of passage into middle age, he thought, since up to now, he had always had a plethora of self-deprivations he could offer in moments when panic slammed him past reason and back into the babbling bargains with the Almighty which had seen him through childhood.

" . . . that Renaissance men were educated to within an inch of their lives and were producing *disciplined* works of art by their early twenties, because they had been ferrying pots of red ochre or whatever for Old Masters since they were in nappies."

Feargal reached out and patted his sister on the back of her head.

"I thought it was yellow ochre."

"Ground-up eggshells or some bloody thing."

"And they had to grind the eggshells by hand, probably, too."

She looked huffy at the mockery. So he went further.

"In fact, if the truth were known, Renaissance man probably served an apprenticeship that involved him standing with his hand cupped underneath the hen, ready to catch each emerging egg."

"Oh, shut up, you. I've missed you, you know."

All in the same tone of voice. That very aggressive affection which made her such a good mother. She could TCP a cut, pull off a dirtied Elastoplast, or cut through a tantrum like no other mother he had ever seen. Fifteen years ago had probably been her best time, he thought, when she had babies and theories and nobody around her of an age to slide away from her tightly packaged precepts.

" . . . the thought of it. I'd rather be dead."

He had no idea what the alternative to death was, in this instance, but it was the idea of death that attracted his attention. His raised level of sensitivity to comments of that nature reminded him of times when Brian, who was blind, had visited the Chelsea apartment.

Everybody would say things to Brian like "did you see so-and-so?" then realise what they had said and be disturbed by it even though Brian, with a lifetime using as valid currency the language of the sighted, was completely undisturbed.

" . . . I would. I'd rather be stone dead."

Stone dead, he thought. That would be a good kind of dead. The kind of dead he dreaded was a seeping, suppurating, putrefying dead, with damp decay and sweet-scented rottenness and waxy strips of flesh sagging away from strait of bone.

"Sing to me."

"Sing what?"

"Drink to me only."

For a second, he needed to think of where to pitch it so she could take the melody and he could improvise around the light soprano voice. Throat-clearing. More throat-clearing.

Faltering start and then the two voices filled the car. They had always sung the songs of a generation before their own; the commonplace of a family where every party was a sing-song.

His sister's voice came out of her, innocent and uninflected as when she was twelve.

Innocent, uninflected and soaring to the high notes without shrillness or stridency. The middle-aged face of her and the speckling of unaltered grey in her hair, and this voice, untouched by time, experience and proudly-claimed moral certitudes.

They finished the song and were silent. She looks upset, his commentator nudged. Better not to ask why. If you ask why, other people's problems seep into the fabric of your time like dye leaking from a garment. You can never get it out of your life, and you can never get it back into their life, so do not invite the sharing of miseries.

A wave of terror, unrelated to her driving, washed over him, and he wanted to scream.

Except, said the commentator, screaming don't achieve nothin'. As a child, he had daydreamed on the swing in the back garden. Always nightmares. Nightmares playing out behind his round face. Nightmares running like a film in his mind, in the hope that if he replayed them enough, he would find a solution to each of them.

There was the death-by-drowning nightmare. The holding of the breath and praying for a hand to reach down into the water and pull him up, his face swelling, blood pounding in his ears as the lungs fought the sphincter of his throat. At ten, at twelve, he had sat on his own and imagined the unspeakable sensation of thick water bloating into nose and mouth. He had read the books that said you would die quickly. Five minutes. But five minutes was not quick. All hell could be experienced in five minutes. Five minutes would go on and on into eternity.

Unknown to him his father had watched his only son and been thankful for the apparent tranquillity of the child. So much better, his father had thought, than if the boy had picked up his mother's nerves. Unknown to his father, the calm-faced child, dreaming in the garden, had all the while been bargaining with terror. Dear God, let me not die by drowning, let me die any way but not by drowning, preferably by a tree falling on me and knocking me unconscious straight away or maybe in my sleep. Dear God, I will give you ten years of my life if you'll just show me now how I'll die. Dear God, I wouldn't mind having both legs amputated and bleeding to death, because bleeding, you would drift away from the pain. But not drowning, please, God.

Marion's voice pulled at his attention.

"Do you hate the thought of going back to the Department?"

"Not really. I've learned a lot. It'll be different."

"Do you go back to the same job?"

"Probably not. Just to the same level."

"Could you have stayed away longer?"

"Probably could have got another extension. That's the beauty of career breaks."

"Not to mention being able to get back in without a medical."

It winded him like a head-butt in the stomach. For a moment, he looked straight ahead, reading the specifications off the back of the artic ahead of their car. Then he looked at her.

Then back at the artic.

"Oh, let's be clear, everybody at home will decide you're fitter than you ever were. You don't have to worry about *that*."

His mouth was fluffily dry and abruptly he was as disconnected, mentally and physically, as when he had first learned to drive, and had been unable to coordinate pushing in the clutch and changing the gear. He had learned to drive in a Mini, all other cars thereafter had felt crowded in their interior – crowded by contrast with the bare-floored front of the Mini.

"Who was the man who invented the Mini?"

"Alec Issigonis," she said without skipping a beat. It was one of the reasons she had done nearly as well as he had in exams, this eerie capacity to retrieve stored information.

His breathing slowed to near-normal in the aftermath of the answer, and he flexed his fingers to unclench them, waiting for her to fill the silence.

"How far is it gone?"

"Pretty far."

"I figured it was hospital, not holidays. You always sent

cards when you went on holidays."

She passed the artic and he found he missed the little block of figures from its back. Tare something, it had said.

"How did you know?"

"I've always known."

No, no, his commentator muttered. That wasn't what I was asking you. I was asking you how you knew I was sick, not how you knew I was gay.

"I wasn't good enough to be *told*, but I've always known."

The bitterness of the reproach hung between them: unprecedented apostasy. The gentle collusion of long-accepted pretences bleached out in a headlong harshness.

Feargal sat, mulled and dumb, no longer fearful of the road.

"I wasn't good enough to be *told*," she repeated.

Feargal made a noise without meaning.

"I was too goddamn provincial and smalltown and *limited*, wasn't I? I mean, you always need someone to make the tea, but your only sister isn't good enough for anything more than making the tea."

The car was now travelling so fast that the soft sleety rain was splattered against the windscreen. Her hand slashed at the windscreen wiper wand and the wipers came on at their fastest speed, flailing at the spreading drops.

"*That* only happens in Dublin and London, dopes from our little neck of the woods wouldn't be able to cope with it. Wouldn't have the sensitivity. Wouldn't *realise*."

The white letters on the speedometer indicative of one tenth of each mile traversed were leaping upwards in jerky movement, the black letters indicative of each complete mile moving more sedately. But not much more sedately. One mile. Another mile. A third mile passed. And another decision made itself for Feargal.

"I'm sorry," he said.

First time in your life you've ever made an unconditional apology, his commentator observed, resuming its discourse without emotion. Up to now, you've always hedged your bets with apologies. "If you understood me to mean X, I'm sorry, I really meant Y." That's the kind of apology you used to make. "I'm sorry if I hurt you", you used to say. As if the hurt was a matter for debate, and you were just issuing a credit note, drawn on your sensibilities, to cover all eventualities.

"I'm very sorry."

The speedometer continued to chop up the miles.

"The day Roger died, I rang you. You were in Dublin that time. This male voice answered and then you came on and Jesus, you started explaining him *away* . . . As if I *cared* . . . I rang you in desperation. My brother would know what to do. Roger was sitting with his legs crossed in the goddam deckchair, *dead*, and you're at the end of a telephone pretending not to be gay, I mean who gave a shit?"

"In the deckchair?"

"Mmm. Going out to tell him his tea was ready and he not moving. Not moving. And not knowing for sure, because the sun had kept him warm. Imagine that. The sun kept him warm. Thinking stupid things – like how could he die on me and me after putting scallions in his salad. Half the time I didn't put scallions in his salad, because I didn't like the smell. How could he die on me without saying goodbye? I shouted at him. I begged him not to be dead. Anything for him not to be dead. I held his hand so tight I left these dents on it. But I couldn't *affect* him, you know?"

Feargal nodded, facing the road, not looking at her.

"It's surprising how few people you can ring up to say 'would you mind taking over, my husband's just died in the deckchair.'"

The sureness had been washed out of her voice by tears. Feargal gestured towards the hard shoulder.

"Pull over. Go on, pull over."

The car drifted, almost of its own volition, over the yellow line and onto the gravel of the hard shoulder. It moseyed aimlessly along the hard shoulder until he pulled up the handbrake and joggled the gearstick into neutral. She held the top of the steering wheel and her face went down on the back of her hands.

"Even the doctor. Hanrahan's locum. More or less said why was I bothering him? Obviously thought I should have said 'OK, Roger, you're dead, we'll get the police or the movers or somebody.' I expected him to carry Roger in. I really did. But he didn't. It was important, to get him in. I was afraid flies would settle on him."

It came out in a howl, and the weight of her head on her arms depressed the centre of the steering wheel, so that the horn bellowed, too. Feargal gently tried to pull her off the wheel and onto his shoulder. She resisted fiercely.

"You came home for two days. Two days. You visited me like a stranger. I needed you to be my pal, my brother, my supporter, but you were so damn busy getting out and away and back to anonymity. You just left me alone, in the dark, strung out between here and eternity with nothing but stale cake and the deckchair and two little bewildered boys. You weighed me up against your privacy and you found me wanting. And you put it down to sensitivity."

She leaned her hot face against the window beside her and cried as if Roger had died yesterday, not eight years before. Gradually the explosive sobs subsided.

"You know, someone brought over his clothes from the golf club. You know that? Dumped them out in the porch. So when I went out to put the milk bottles out, there they were, a pile of his clothes, not washed, smelling of him. Five weeks after he died."

Passing juggernauts rocked the car on its wheels. Feargal got out of his side and walked to the driver's door. Marion scrambled across the middle of the car and huddled in the passenger seat. He got in, fastened the seat-belt and made to put the key in the ignition.

Glanced at her. Waited.

"I don't know how I knew you were sick. Or when. I just knew."

"Me, too."

"Sorry?"

"Before I had symptoms, I knew. One day, I just knew. The test was no surprise."

"You're on millions of pills."

It wasn't a question.

"Yes."

"I've been reading up about it. Night sweats and stuff."

"Why?"

"Why what?"

"Why would you be reading up about it?"

She looked at him as if the answer were so obvious that the question must be facetious.

"Because I'll have to look after you."

He was suddenly furious.

"Says who, for fuck's sake?"

"Says me."

It was said with such simplicity that a blanket of calm and inevitability fell.

Feargal looked out at the darkening sky. The rain had stopped. Except when the big lorries were passing, it was quiet. The inside of the car felt clammy to him.

"I'm good at it and you don't want to be among strangers. Among *professionals*."

She's right, his commentator told him. Absolutely right. She's as strong as a little bull. With neither revulsion nor pride in the wiping and debriding. It must be done, therefore she must do it. That's the way it's always been. Duty follows her. She is someone to make the tea. Someone to manage the dying.

"Manage the dying," he said aloud, and the terror washed in again, but at a lower level, like the incoming wave of a receding tide.

"Easier than Roger."

"Because I'm not your husband?"

"No. Lord, no." She was surprised. "You'll be able to go through the rage and the fear and the pain and get through to a peaceful place where there's no hope. Not hurled into it like being driven into a wall."

He considered this for a moment.

"You may be a natural nurse, but as a saleswoman, you're crap, you know that?"

She laughed unsteadily.

"Don't discourage me. I'll have to sell it to Ma and Da in due course."

He started the car and turned the lights on, moving off the hard shoulder and onto the main road again.

"D'you know what I'd like?" she asked, her tone back to normal.

"What would you like?"

"Chips. There's a takeaway in the next town."

"You never lost it."

"Nah. Everybody but me knows where pubs or churches are. Me, I know every chipper and Chinese in this country."

He drove steadily and skilfully in the gathering darkness, watching for the bright red Coca-Cola signs over the chip shop. Its window was sweated with condensation.

"What do you want?"

She was rooting in her handbag for her purse.

"A single. No vinegar."

"Rubbish. You need protein. You're having a burger."

The door slammed behind her and she stumped into the shop.

It was ever thus, his commentator observed. Kindness and coercion. Blood brothers. Soul sisters.

He examined the proposition and was content with it.

Butterfly Christmas

He had marched the Christmas trees out to where she sat in the car. Two by two, thumping their stumps into the pavement and twirling them. The first two she rejected.

"Spacer," she said decidedly, then shook her head as a wet dog does, two rigid hands rising off her lap to sketch in the air.

"Spacer," she said again, helplessly.

A couple of passers-by, one clutching two turkeys by the neck in much the same way as her husband held the trees, stopped to watch.

"Bigger around?" her husband asked. She was silent.

"Taller?"

The nod was frantic.

"No problem," he said, and marched the shorter trees away.

The chosen tree was now anchored in a clever red contraption that held water, and five sets of tiny lights had been threaded all over it. Today, he would put up the decorations. She went to turn in the bed and failed. The reflexes of mobility don't give up easily, she reflected. Nor the dreams filled with unplanned, unquestioned movement.

"Very fortunate your ribs weren't broken," he said, sliding out of his side of the bed and heading for the bathroom. "You'd never have managed without the deep sighs."

Snorting laughter overcame her, alone in the big bed. The snorts had been there since childhood, but in self-conscious adolescence she had developed the habit of cupping a hand over mouth and nose so that her laughter made a drowned noise.

Now, neither hand could reach mouth and nose. Thinking about this provoked an itch beside her nostril. She concentrated on it, having been taught that if you tried to make it get worse rather than better, you could eventually make it go away. Your brain lost interest in paying so much attention to one small irritant.

The itch stayed and worsened, unaware of the sophisticated psychology being applied to it. It took ownership of her as pain never had. In the intensive care unit, staff had driven her berserk by their solicitude for the pain. Pain control was now in fashion. Everybody was geared to stop it before it started, as opposed to the old days when it was allowed to become a raging torrent before the easing needle was employed. Nobody, however, was geared to take an itch seriously. And for her, the itches were worse than the pain.

He was beside her with a rough dry face cloth. He rubbed it impersonally all over her face, scouring the itch away. The cloth then went into the bowl of hot water he had carried in, its coarse terry loops softening so that when he washed her face, it was a warm wet infusion of comfort.

"This is gonna hurt you more than it hurts me," he said, as he now always did, before cleaning her teeth.

The jaws were locked, leaving only an inch of access. The brush, scrubbing against the enamel, was loud in her ears as he talked to her, the words lost. She looked a question at him, but he seemed contented with her lack of response, and dressed her, buttoning her blouse right up to the collar as if readying her in a school uniform.

"I've solved the problem of getting you downstairs," he said, as he looped one of her arms over his shoulder and lifted her. As he carried her across the small landing, she could feel the redness rising in her face for shame at her own heaviness.

"Now I'm going to lean you against the wall and slide you down," he said, ignoring her anxious grunts.

The painted wall was smooth and chill against the white blouse as he slid her down to a sitting position at the top of the stairs where he had laid the single bed duvet. Once she was seated, he pulled the plaster rigidities of her legs out in front of her, pointing down the stairs towards where he was, a few steps below her. He tipped her forward so that her head was on his shoulder, and gently pulled the duvet, so that her bottom went bump from one step to another, her forehead hitting the soft padded shoulder of his cardigan in an off-tempo echo. She began to laugh at the awkward efficiency of it, sucking in hairs from the cardigan at every in-breath.

Three steps from the bottom he straightened her up as briskly as if she had been a shop-mannequin, and hefted her into the wheelchair.

"*Now*," he said, kicking off the brake of the wheelchair with enormous satisfaction. "Now."

He parked her where she could watch the flames of the freshly-lit fire and went off to the other end of the long oblong room to start making breakfast. She could follow what he was doing by the sounds. Paper rustling and then a clunk as sliced bread was slid into a toaster.

A fainter click as the kettle went on. Cracking of eggshells and the chatty monologue of an egg frying. He always fried eggs too quickly so they developed a lacework of bubbles and a black edge.

"Oh, d'you know what . . . " he said, coming over to the stereo and rifling through discs.

"What would you like?"

"Diminished fifth," she said. Quite clearly. He looked at her in intense silence, a record in one hand, a teatowel flung over his shoulder.

"Minor Detail?" he suggested. She nodded, wondering again at the scrambled brain cells that could so transpose a band's name. He put on the disc and returned to the cooking, swearing to himself as the fat spat at him.

He had developed a way of feeding the two of them, mouthful about, which ensured that both got hot food, but which required concentration on both parts. He got momentarily touchy when she turned her head away from a proffered bite of toast.

She was looking beyond him at the window of the converted eighteenth-century millhouse.

"Butterflies," she said. The word was muffled but unmistakeable. Her husband sat back in his chair and went through his usual routine.

"Butter? No. Marmalade? Birds? Decorations? Music?"

"Butterflies," she said again, more firmly.

"Jesus, I can't figure . . . " he said, baffled.

She butted her head in the direction she wanted him to look, but he was back with the problem of food.

"I'll work it out in a minute, OK?" he said, and inserted toast in her mouth as if he was a postman delivering a letter. For a moment, she considered shoving it back out with her tongue, but sucked it instead. The next time he arrived with a forkful of black lacy egg she turned her head as far away as she could.

"OK," he said, ostentatiously patient. "OK. Butterflies."

He stood up, turned to the window, and a coloured cloud of them surrounded him. Some of them settled on him, the elaborate primary colours bright against the grey of his cardigan.

He stood in startled stillness.

"Butterflies," he said again, his accent adding a soft aitch after the T so they became buttherflies. There were at least ten of them. He nudged the one on his shoulder and it shifted to the back of his hand. He brought it to her, placing it on the frame that held her wrist rigid. For a few seconds, the russet and ultramarine wings fluttered anxiously, and then were at peace. She watched it for a long time in silence, rehearsing the words so they would come out right.

"At Christmas?"

The man nodded.

"Never heard of that before. Maybe because it's thatched. Maybe the eggs got laid and the warmth of the fire . . . "

He poked the one on his arm until it flew off and settled on the Christmas tree, and then put a fire guard in front of the flames. The room was warmer now and the butterflies flew high in the rafters as if in the branches of a tree in midsummer. She wanted to look more closely at the one on her wrist but could bring it no closer.

"Tantalus," she said aloud.

"Yeah," her husband said, picking up the plates and heading for the sink.

Not being able to get a proper view of the butterfly tainted the pleasure of it being there at all, she realised. It was like having eye-floaters, those oddly-shaped images that stay constantly out of visual range, rising and falling with the pattern of one's gaze. Tantalus and the grapes. Or was it grapes? Water, perhaps? And what had been the offence for which that perverse incarceration was the punishment? Her ideas floated ahead of her like a conveyor-belt clothes-line decorated with pegs, but moving too fast for garments to be appended thereto. A moment of misery surged inside her head, pressing against the hard shell of her skull as the traumatised brain had.

"Tantalus," she said, more exigently.

"I know bugger all about Tantalus," he said comfortably, clattering clean plates. "Nothin'. Empty. White sheet."

Catching the demand in her face, he closed his eyes to dredge for memories.

"I presume Tantalus is the guy who gave rise to the word tantalise," he speculated. "Same as yer man that couldn't push the stone up the hill. Sisyphus. Tantalus had some equivalently frustrating exercise that he couldn't quite fulfil. I'll look it up in the library when we go out."

She sat silently, the front of her legs beginning to be too warm in the fire-heat. He would not remember to look it up, she knew, and she would not remember to remind him. And if she later reproached him, he would laugh and tell her he had more important things to be doing.

"Now, tell me where these go," he said, kicking off the wheelchair brake and pushing her towards the Christmas tree. Her legs cooled down and she nodded her instructions as to where the tinsel baubles should go. Pain was riveting the bones of her face.

"Don't grind your teeth. Makes you look like Desperate Dan in the Dandy," he said.

She watched him open two capsules and empty them into a flat soupspoon filled with yogurt.

He fed the sour mixture to her and a great shudder at the taste ran through her, knocking her plastered legs together and forcing one rigid forearm off the arm of the wheelchair. He lifted the arm back into position without comment.

Nor did he make predictions about the painkiller, as her mother would have done.

"You'll feel the good of that in just a few minutes," her mother would always say. "You'll never notice the time passing."

Having dosed her as neatly as a farmer dosing a sheep, he went off to get logs, stepping into wellington boots at the door before heading out into the rainy backyard. For a moment she was filled with fear that the butterflies would follow him out the open door and wilt in the cold outside air, but they stayed where they were. He came back to build up the fire with the sure-handed enjoyment he took in any physical task. He sat back on his hunkers, his hands palmed towards the blaze.

Then the boots were shoved off and he heel-padded in socked feet to wash his hands. One of the butterflies settled on the hot tap, and he tipped it with the back of his hand to get it away.

"Needn't have bothered our arses buying decorations," he said, half to himself. "Free butterflies . . . "

The pain was beginning to ease, keeping in time with her pulse as it retreated.

"Here," he said. "Hold these."

The lightness of the box put into her lap mimicked paper. She pushed with her caged hand at the lid until it came up and off and fell to the floor. The sound of it was swamped in a sudden loud rigour of Gregorian chant from the record player. Her husband's voice joined those of the choir.

"*Lumen ad revelationem gentium* . . . "

Six bright silver balls sat, segregated, egg-fashion, in the box, reflecting back six fattened faces at her. Bloated by the convex mirroring, the face was nonetheless different, nose tilted at an angle, forehead dented, the dent rimmed by pale raised scarring. A squealing whimper came through her clenched teeth and the six reflections blurred. Her husband, unhearing, came back to the wheelchair, still singing, and began – deftly – to loop skinny wire hooks onto the baubles.

"Jesus," he said, breaking off from the male voices. "Don't *dribble* on the bloody things. Oh. You're crying. Why're you crying?"

The caged hand thumped against her chin, then on to the baubles. The voices continued to sing "*Nunc dimittis servum tuum, domine*".

"Your face, is it?"

She nodded. He mopped her with the tea towel from off his shoulder.

"Yeah," he said thoughtfully, taking some of the hooked baubles and beginning to position them on the tree. "I'd forgotten you wouldn't have seen yourself since the accident."

His tone was casually observant, as if commenting on a one-degree change in external temperature or the lateness of a newspaper. She roared at him in wordless agony, bubbles forming and bursting in the gap between top and bottom teeth. He finished hanging the baubles, came back and mopped her again.

"You have a thing called keloid scarring," he said informatively. "That's why the bump on your head has a kind of a rim on it. If you really want to, later, you can have it sort of filed down. But probably if you just grew your fringe a bit longer . . . Other than that, your face is going to be a bit different. But you'll get used to it. I have."

He took the now empty box off her lap and replaced it with another one. When the lid came off, it was filled with red balls, crusted with metallic grains and non-reflective. After a moment, he resumed the Gregorian chant. When the track ended, he hummed the notes again.

"Good singer always hits the notes from above," he said, quoting some college music teacher he had liked. "Never *reaches* for them . . . "

You are without sympathy, she thought. You are without imagination. You lack the capacity to understand the true horror of being behind a strange distorted face, of knowing that it will never present to the outside world what you are used to it presenting. You have no patience for "talking out" of problems and your favourite phrase is "there's the status quo, and there's worse – which do you want?". You have already got used to my battered face and you will never understand why I should have a problem doing the same. It wouldn't even occur to you to say that you see my face more than I do: you simply don't empathise enough to argue it through at all.

"D'you know what I was thinking?" her husband was standing over her, dangling a red bauble from its hook. One of the butterflies had settled on it. "We won't be able to have candles at all. And we'll have to be very careful with the toaster and things like that. I must rig a couple of shields to prevent these lads from getting into danger."

She held out her arms to him and he put his head down on her neck, one arm extended to take care of the butterfly. In a desperation of trust and need, she hugged him awkwardly, hiding her hospital-pale face in the always tanned warm skin of his neck.

"Now," he said, straightening up as if something had been settled and returning to the task.

"Butterflies and Christmas. What more could we want?"

Notice of Redundancy

Under the category of "Half-remembered" in my mind is a snippet about prostitutes who suffered some congestive ailment in their genitals because they were constantly aroused but rarely experienced orgasm. It's possible I have the same ailment all over me, through rage constantly provoked, never vented.

I am everybody's best friend. I am the keeper of the secrets. I am the one who sits, watching, while women walk the room, tears and rhetorical questions spewing sideways out of them the way sweat-drops spew from characters in cartoons.

"How could he *do* that to me?" they ask, knowing I will not hang an unwelcome answer on the hook of their question mark.

"What kind of thing is that to say?" they demand.

When they fling themselves onto my little couch and weep, they do not know that the very couch is there, chosen for this purpose, not for hurly-burly. I know the moves like an old hoofer. Fat women must be held gently by both shoulders, never lower down. Those extremes of misery which cause pinpointed headaches at the forehead's centre like an Indian's diamond require a warm palm planted above the eyebrows, holding in the pain.

They tell me things they don't tell others and they tell me their wonder at their self-revelation.

"I don't know why I'm saying all this to you," they say, in transient moments of doubt. My hand feathers the air in self-dismissal and they resume centre-stage as if it was their proper place. It is easy for them to consign me to the wings, to the prompter's box. Always has been. Gaze at the school photographs of a few years' back and your eye is drawn to the glowing certainties of the nascent beauties, or to the impatient arrogance of the clever ones, or to the spark-eyed malevolent glee of the ones who will go through life attended by the whiff of sulphur. Me – I am one of the dough-faced make-weights in between the eye-pullers. I am the canvas on which the bright splotches of their lives are thrown.

It has always been thus, and I am comfortable with it, knowing my role. I am a witness at other lives, hands at the ready to applaud the breakthroughs of individual members of the sisterhood, shoulder braced for the sustenance and succour of the temporarily stricken.

There's not much competition for the role I play. The job specification requires a physical appearance which is unspectacular in its unattractiveness. "Best friends" are never startling in their good looks or ugliness: one must not distract from another's drama. A safe plainness, the kind the Americans call 'homely', is the optimum. Pale, pear-shaped and grey-eyed, I define the standard. As I do in my relationships. It would not do to step outside the counterpoint category by tempestuous tantrums or by scalding affairs with men sleek-hided and elegant in their moves. It would not do, and it does not happen. Like calls to like. Species knows species.

Given that nobody competes for my post as supportive spectator, I was taken aback when Treena suggested a joint visit to Hilary Nestor. I suppose I'm not good enough, the huffy sub-text in my mind said, while my mouth produced the non-judgemental clarifiers at which I am so practised.

"What an interesting idea," I said neutrally. "Are you clear on what you can achieve that way?"

"I just feel it might . . . " Treena answered, inflecting it as if it were a completed thought. "You know?"

"Go on," I said carefully, taking the coffee flask and heading for the hob. I serve a lot of flavoured coffee but have suspected for some time that it may be a social error. This evening, the flavouring was Bailey's Irish Cream. The scent as the steam hit the second instalment of grounds was as ambiguous and tame as the smell of baby food.

"Just, she's got this fantastic reputation. Jane Stephenson talks about her all the time. Jane says she gets people out of their own way."

Jane would, I thought, wouldn't she? Jane lives in a world of pasteurised insights and one-liners. Her apartment has a bookshelf unit filled with self-improvement books from the seventies. White-covered paperbacks, their brown-edged pages showing age, primary colour assertions and exhortations undefeated in their promises of a thinner, happier, more assertive, immeasurably more orgasmic future. Each one in its time was, for perhaps half a year, the crampon Jane ratcheted into the icy wall of the unknown. And used to raise herself a little higher.

"Get people out of their own way?" I repeated, ready to pour coffee into clean replacement cups. (I keep Milton liquid in my kitchen to ensure that my coffee cups never develop ochre staining and even though I rinse them obsessively, I'm always worried that the disinfectant taste will come through.)

"Will you come with me when I go to see her?"

The question came back like an answer.

"Why – why would you need me?"

"Just."

Just. It wrote *finis* to the discussion the way an extra fat full stop puts an end to an article in a magazine.

So one week later, we were ushered in to Hilary Nestor's office. We smiled at the receptionist and the secretary, denied, then confirmed, the need for coffee, deferred to each other in the selection of chairs.

How big she was startled me. Television appearances had falsified the scale of her. The strong handshake was delivered by a large, unadorned hand. She outranked the two of us in height, a height added to by tall-heeled shoes. The vividness of her sucked the oxygen out of the air I was breathing. Coarse short hair, russetted with dye into a statement of conscious artificiality. Art Deco earrings. Colours that might have come off the covers of the "how to" books.

The big hands went down on the round table that served her as a desk and fanned out flat, as if clearing the already clear space.

"OK. What's the objective this morning?"

The glance went from Treena to me, and Treena followed it, looking at me as if I might speak. I nodded the initiative to her.

"Well, Jane Stephenson sings your praises," she began. "She says you've done wonderful things for her."

"Oh, yes, Jane. Jane gave me that," Hilary Nestor said, turning over a triangular wooden display piece that read *A Woman's Place is in Command*. It had been lying, message concealed, in the corner. She made no further comment on Jane and expected none. Treena cranked herself up for further speech.

"It's really me, more than Claire here," she said. "I just thought we might talk around an issue that's causing me – that's in my life at the moment."

"No."

At that moment the coffee arrived. Bowl-like cups in Prussian blue, daubed with contrast colours embossed so that the pads of one's fingers met with mounded glaze. Hilary Nestor took her cup and waited until we had taken ours. We refused the Belgian biscuits, although we wanted them, notching up positives for ourselves on the ever-running calorie scoresheet.

Hilary took two of the biscuits, setting them side by side on the desk.

"Never mind a better mousetrap. The world will beat a path to the door of whoever invents a saucer that lets you put chocolate biscuits on it without them melting all over the cup," she commented.

The door closed behind the coffee-bringer. Hilary Nestor did the table-fanning gesture again.

"Let's get it clear right from the start, Treena," she said. "We're not friends. I'm sure you've loads of friends, but I'm not one of them. I'm a hired gun. You're going to pay me money for this session. You're *not* going to pay me £125 to 'talk around an issue'. That's what you do with friends. So start again. What's the objective? What are you going to achieve here this morning?"

The collective plural had become a directive singular. I wondered if that was a device to diminish my importance. I wondered, too, why I thought of Treena in first name terms, but of Hilary Nestor in both first and second name, as if she were a public event like the Grand National.

Treena laughed lightly. Hilary Nestor looked blankly at her.

"Well," Treena began, "I feel that I could probably do with some help, right enough, because I probably haven't coped that well – "

"No."

The big red-haired woman repeated it like a garda's ultimatum: out of that car right now and hands on the roof.

"Your objective. What do you want out of this morning?"

The blush surged over Treena's prominent collar bones, marbling her cheeks with purplish heat. There was silence. Hilary Nestor waited.

"I want to win out over a son of a bitch who's screwing me, every move I make."

The blurt was so loud she put a hand to her mouth at the end of it.

Hilary Nestor put her head on one side.

"Screwing you?"

The tone was silky, amused. Treena laughed like a cramp relaxing.

"No, not sexually. No, he's not like that."

"What *is* he like? Who is he, for starters?"

The story fell out in clumps of fury and illustration, chronology awry. He was Treena's boss, in a big multinational corporation. Not likely to be promoted further, probably already at his point of stasis, parked a notch or two past his level of competence. A limited man, but limitless in his sycophancy and his self-defensive plotting. His superiors had used Treena on a couple of tasks because of a specialist knowledge she had, and the process threatened him. He had taken to following her around. He wanted reports on everything done and said. Had fed her lines to say at the next meeting and had gone lip-narrowing silent when he subsequently found she hadn't said them. Had peddled his own views, unsought, to his superiors and had turned rancid when those views met with unexplained disregard. His own job one of delegation and trifling detail, he had funnelled his energies into ritual humiliations of Treena. Memos were carefully cc'd to everybody at her level but her. Items were sent directly to her assistants, without her having sight of them.

"He didn't even invite me to the Christmas drinks party

in his office. I didn't know what to do, so I went in anyway and he looked through me. He asked the person beside me what she'd like to drink but never asked me. Everybody saw it. Everybody. I mean, the *signal* it sent out . . . "

"What did you do?"

"I just stood there. What *could* I do?"

"What did you do afterwards?"

"I went to him and asked him was anything I was doing unsatisfactory."

"And?"

"And he said why would I ask that, my annual review was on file and I knew it had found me satisfactory."

"And?"

"And I said, 'Well, *something* I'm doing must be wrong, because I sense – I just get the feeling that you're not really happy with me,' you know?"

"Mmm?" The interrogative mumble came through chocolate biscuit being chewed.

"Well, he just said he didn't know why I'd have that impression. And I said . . . the vibrations."

"Sorry?"

"I said . . . the vibrations. The vibes were negative. The vibes from him. And he just repeated that he didn't know why I would have that impression. He was fiddling with his pen and so I just said I was glad to hear it and thank you and came out of his office. And after that it got worse."

"How?"

"Just. At meetings, he would ask my opinion so formally it was like he was asking a child a grown-up's question and everybody could read the signals and see I was being . . . " Treena's gesture was evocative of being trivialised, marginalised.

"So, what do you want from me?"

Hilary Nestor's question came like a smack in the face. Smack-startled tears filled Treena's eyes. I reached out to touch her.

"Don't do that."

The instruction was tonelessly authoritarian: do that stuff on your own time, not during my chargeable hour, not on my premises. I dithered and withdrew. The silence was as absolute as silence ever is in a city. Outside laughter leaked around the door. A car alarm somewhere shrieked its Johnny-one-note hysteria.

The first wave of silence retreated. Hilary Nestor ate the second biscuit methodically, breaking it into three pieces first, and, afterward, sweeping the crumbs onto the floor. Some nameless slave would come and clean them up.

"I want you to tell me what to do."

"In order to what?"

"I don't understand?"

"I can tell you how to get another job or I can tell you how to beat him. Which do you want?"

"Tell me how to beat him."

I couldn't take it any more.

"I would have to question your approach."

The statement came out of me covered in self-conscious pomposity, of a piece with phrases like "do not hesitate to ask" and "with all due respect".

"Yes?"

The big painted face turned to me, gaudy and sure of itself as a sunflower.

"The notion that you might impose a solution from outside or provide methods – surely Treena must be facilitated to her own – "

"Beat him," Treena repeated, rolling over the end of my sentence. "I want to stay put and I want to beat him. Tell me how to do that."

The sunflower turned to the new source of raised temperature.

"OK."

She pushed a pad of memo sheets across the table to Treena. Her own name topped every sheet in a simple serif typeface. No logo. Treena took out her floral Parker and uncapped it.

"For starters, get the hell rid of that pen."

Treena looked at the pretty pen in astonishment.

"A pen is a tool of business, not a cutesy-pie personal adornment."

I checked the mug holding pens on the table. Clear plastic BICs, two matt black Parkers and a few neon highlighters.

"Get rid of the Dewberry, too," Hilary Nestor added. "Swear off the Body Shop. Either wear no perfume or something with a little subtlety. Get rid of the fob."

This I didn't follow until I noticed Treena nervously fiddling with the little gold stick at the end of her necklet. Fob? Is that what it was?

"Every second woman wears a fob," Hilary Nestor said dismissively.

I felt a moment's surge of inappropriate relief. I don't smell of Dewberry and I don't own a fob.

"Sit up straight. *Look* at you."

We all did. Treena was seated, legs wound around each other, hands clenched between her knees, tilted forward. A humbled Oliver asking for more.

"Learn to displace air. Create an expectation at a meeting that your contribution will be significant. Don't crawl into a room hoping to be liked. You're a professional woman. Being liked is a side issue."

The flowered Parker flew over the little square sheets, obediently noting every dictum.

"And change your language."

This one was delivered with the added vigour you invest in something you know will meet with resistance.

"Don't introduce everything you say with 'I feel'. Who

cares what you feel? In business terms, all that matters is data. So when you're disagreeing, give the data first and then the point. Like this: 'Given the fall-off in the figures for the fourth quarter, it would be unwise to take on new staff'. Not: 'I don't feel we should take on new staff right now'."

She stopped to let the flying hand of the note-taker catch up with her and looked out the window. The car alarm had been silenced.

"No modifiers. None of this 'maybe we should' stuff. Men make statements. Women make pleadings."

Both Treena and I started to talk together. Hilary Nestor watched us as we kowtowed ourselves into mutually resentful silences.

"What you're saying is we should talk like men," I said.

"That's a crude summary, but in essence, yes."

"But we are *women*. We have our own culture, our own heritage, our own identity, our own language. We think differently. We behave differently. We have different values. Little girls are more cooperative with each other than little boys. They bend the rules in order to share the winning. Men are much more confrontational and competitive. They talk of winning and losing, not of feelings or of learning. Why should we abandon all of that, sell it out? Surely we should be trying to change the way *men* talk and think in the interests of creating a better world?"

Treena looked at me for seconds after I finished speaking, and in her attention, I felt the tilt of consent moving in my direction.

"It is a legitimate point," she said to Hilary Nestor, and I felt gratitude and fury. Gratitude at the description, fury at the fair-minded way she was presenting it to Hilary Nestor, who was already nodding.

"Absolutely," the woman conceded. "Let us all strive to

be better Christians."

I gestured for clarity.

"Your point is well taken. It is quite legitimate. It is worthy. It is pointless. We women are entering occupied territory. The priority is to take the territory, not to convert the occupiers in advance."

"But you're talking as if it was a *war*," I said. "You're talking as if you were a man, turning Treena into another man."

"Look," the big sunflower woman said gently. "This is all very interesting stuff for a consciousness-raising session where everybody trades inadequacies and vulnerabilities. But it doesn't solve problems. I'm going to give Treena directions and if she wants to *win* as opposed to just doing shared feminist whingeing, then she'll follow them."

Unspoken was the addendum: and you (meaning me) aren't paying anything. You are a prop in this production and you should shut up. I did. Her directions came thick and fast. The strategy for bypassing the boss and tying herself into his superiors. The tactics for keeping him constantly confused, yet flattered. The *modus operandi* for extending tentacles into other Departments.

"Oh, *networking*," Treena said brightly at this point, adapting to the teacher-pupil relationship.

"No, *not* networking," Hilary Nestor said. "Networking is women talking about empowerment and pledging mutual support, which, given the low levels women have reached in management, isn't worth a damn. It's just a non-alcoholic version of AA."

The words continued, sucked in by Treena's pen and noted in unquestioned soundbites. I sat, pushing static into my own ears so that I couldn't quite hear her. The hour finished in a flurry of instructions, a firm handshake and a warmly impersonal good wish. We were out in the noon-time streets, wind whipping at our hair, rushing purposefully until we realised I must go in a quite different direction from Treena's. We paused outside the Tea-Time Express, my foot on a bronze quotation from *Ulysses* embedded in the flagstones of the path, and did a fast litany of offers and refusals. Come on in and have a cup of coffee, no time, got to get back, you're a dote to come with me, I can't tell you, no problem, it's a pleasure, I'll ring you before the end of the week . . .

The latter was a kindly lie from Treena. She would not ring me and I knew it. I was suddenly like a photograph in a family album. Black and white and sepia'd with respect, but no match for the glossy, full-colour certitudes of a Hilary Nestor. I had not before thought of the wind of change as the smacking buffet delivered by a passing express train. But that's how it was. My non-directive infinitely supportive counselling had made me as redundant as a rag-picker. Its quiet non-interventionism would leave no trace. As irrationally obedient to an unspoken command as a traveller in an elevator who turns to face the closed doors, I walked into an artist's supply shop and began to choose a new pen. A man ahead of me was making a fuss over a list of items he wanted. I tried out different writing instruments on a pad provided and settled eventually for an Italic felt pen.

As the man forced the assistant to go into the back room for one special requirement after another, I wrote phrases on the pad provided.

"*A witness at other lives,*" I wrote in Victorian cursive script.

The man wanted a 200-sheet refill pad, ruled narrow feint and margin. The assistant tried to persuade him that a margin was not essential. He refused to be persuaded.

Back she went into the store room. I tried block letters on the pad.

"P.45", I wrote.

The shopper ahead of me had one last item on his list, which the assistant, with pleased decisiveness, told him was not in stock and would not be coming back into stock. Within seconds, his goods were checked out, bagged – and he was on his way, peeved over the missing item. The assistant turned to me, and took the Italic pen from me, upending it to read the price label.

"I mean, you'd think I was *hiding* it from him," she said.

I smiled and met her eyes with the old, instinctive, share-it-with-me gaze.

"I mean, let's be honest," she said as she slipped pen and receipt into a tiny paper bag and handed it over. "You don't get much call for blotting-paper these days, do you?"

Intensive Care

We buried the old man today, having tortured him for fifty-three days. We never meant to torture him, but torture him we did. Not personally, mind. We just delivered him to a system where good people had no option but to torture him.

We had promised him, ten years ago, that we wouldn't do it.

That was when they discovered the aneurysm. Below his heart, they told him was this vessel, swollen and stretched out of shape, weakened by distortion. It could blow any time, they said.

Surgery was indicated, they said. Stuff your surgery, he said. I'm taking my chances. I'm seventy. Any kind of major surgery at my age could kill me anyway. Convalescence would drive me mad. It's your choice, they told him, disapproving. He went home.

He lived for eleven years with the billowing vessel. The GP on occasional visits would palpate the area and wonder aloud if surgery shouldn't be reconsidered. The old man never changed his mind. There would be no high-technology, no tubes nor tests. He would not relinquish his life to a hospital and its systems.

He gave orders to us, his sons, now and again. If the

worst happened – let him die. Made us promise him, the two of us present, both as moral checks on each other and as a strengthening of the message. He wrote it down, the same intent, in neat unadorned clerk's handwriting, and put it in a separate compartment in his desk, reminding us, now and again, of its location.

The eyesight went, during those eleven years. A reader, he went first to the big print books in the local library and then to books on tape. But listening to a Fionnuala Flanagan reading Joyce is not the same as hoovering the nuggety rhythms up off the page yourself. The spines of books in the library defeated him, as he stood, not so much squinting as trying to keep his glasses at an angle that had always been effective – by scrunching his cheeks up. Keeping glasses up on cheeks thinned down to bone gave him a tooth-bared rictus.

His life curled back at the edges, that decade. Walking, when you can't see, is no confident enjoyment with thoughts free-floating. Eating is an opportunity for accident and humiliation.

Seventy years of seeing made him expect to see. The failure kept surprising him. He kept telling people of this new discovery.

"It's as if there's a teardrop right down through the centre of my vision," he would explain. "I keep thinking if I can surprise it by getting to one side of the teardrop, I'll be able to see what I'm looking at, but I can't."

After a while, the explanation, new-found to him, caused eye-rolling in the rest of us. Or worse. My brother's son Scott – the only grandson – would see the discovery coming, and would line up beside the old man, a smooth, tanned, orange-juice-and-codliver-oil young version of him. Scott could match his grandfather's tone and gesture to the life. The words, through repetition, would come easily from him.

"It's as if there's a teardrop," the two of them would begin together. The first time Scott did it, a shiver of fear ran through me. I waited for the old man's wrath at the disrespect. But he swiped at his grandson and his grandson hugged him.

Loss of sight, nonetheless, did turn my father's life reactive. The shadows walking towards him on the path took voice before they took shape.

"Hello, Mr Clifford," they would say, and he would give a yellow-pack greeting terse in its un-involvement and walk on, rather than seek re-introduction and identification each time. Every trip to the shops ended as a pitched battle with assistants too busy to spare time and tolerance for an irritable, articulate oul' fella who was always ready to give you an argument about what he couldn't see.

He had always been a gardener. He gardened like a graffiti artist, left no surface undecorated if a clinging vine could be persuaded to take it over. Hanging baskets depended from hooks of all shapes. Bright-coloured flowers were trained over arches, poked through trellises and hung from arbours. Down at the back, he had a little sheltered area where plants were re-potted and ailing shrubs given extra care.

All of this receded from him. He tried to garden by remote control, instructing my mother or young Scott. That was better than nothing, even if the full ungoverned glory of the end result was beyond his vision. Scott developed a knack of reporting what he could see, dressing the reportage up as a question, and though the sharp old man knew damn well what he was up to, he liked it, nonetheless.

During those years, Scott mined a vein of unsentimental generosity in himself that was missing from his own father. My brother Timothy veered daily between humouring the old man and snapping at him. After a time, I noted, he used Scott as his representative. His ambassador. Scott was more equable than Timothy had ever been, but he had no tolerance for the self-indulgences of age, and in pitiless parody joked the old man into jettisoning many of them.

Scott came from a school bus filled with rap and exploratory sex jokes, and he stepped, each afternoon – willingly – into a world of George Burns and Gracie Allen. My father loved Victor Borge, and Scott, at ten, could do a splendid rendition of Borge's punctuation skit. Because my father loved James Plunkett, the boy, at eleven, knew the short story ending with "like an aspirin. Like a bloody big aspirin."

Scott and my father educated each other, too. Scott would talk Harley Davidsons, my father, TT races in the Isle of Man in the 30s. You had to look at the little black and white pictures, because he could tell from the angle of your voice if you were looking at something else or only pretending to pay attention. Timothy often got caught out. Me less frequently. Not because I was more attentive. Just lazier.

Scott would talk school and friends or enemies. My father made no judgements, kept all secrets – the only person in the boy's life who seemed to be able to do either. They had a closed circle of jeering and jubilation. My mother left them to it for the most part. She used their time together to catch up on the tasks the blindness multiplied for her. When Scott wasn't there, she checked on my father as he went about his idly busy day.

I came into their kitchen, one day, to find her leaning on the edge of the sink, wet to the wrists washing dishes. She nodded silently at the window. We watched my father in the garden, as he stood winded, with the tall-handled spade, using its grinding against the paving stones as a guide. A robin came close. He could not see it.

"It breaks my heart," my mother whispered. "Do you

see the way the robin puts its head on one side as if it's puzzled that your father isn't noticing it and chirping at it any more?"

"Anthropomorphic," was Timothy's verdict on this, when I later told him.

"You're quite right," I said cravenly. I understood for the first time why Scott talked so much more freely with his grandfather than with his father.

Pieces of music would push the old man into affection. When an afternoon programme played Bob Hope singing "Thanks . . . for the Memories," my father wanted to dance with my mum in the kitchen. When they played the intermezzo from Cavelleria Rusticana (their wedding music) he was red-eyed.

Mum, whose workload increased in direct ratio to his decremental skill balance, would have to halt and scrabble in her always short supply of nostalgia for an appropriate response.

He had outlived his intellectual enemies. This left him revving a malevolent engine, a gear that would never engage. He was a man born for opposition, a man who spotted an emerging consensus a mile off and whose immediate reaction was to go into kamikaze mode.

As his seventies wore on, Mum sustained his complaints, theories and rhetorical questions. "Would someone kindly explain to me," was the standard opening. But he didn't want an explanation. He wanted a fight. He was surrounded by people too busy or too loving to give him one.

Scott grew, in those same years, from a tubby under-sized pal to a tall witty friend. The old man and the young man met in a place of trust and growth where neither Timothy nor I had ever met our father.

And then the thing blew. Suddenly, he was throwing up and throwing up, and a jagged rift of excruciation ran through the middle of him. My mother called an ambulance, the old suburb had its air split by the siren.

On a trolley, in the hospital, he gasped details to fill questionnaires and begged that the pain be taken away. The surgeon, already capped and greened for action, gently started to explain that until they had identified precisely what was wrong, there was no validity in analgesia.

"Don't fucking lecture me," my father said. The surgeon retreated. Minutes later, the old man went under a morphine cloud ready for surgery. They came to tell my mother and ask her to sign the consent form. He's already in theatre, they said.

"But why?" she cried. "He'd never have wanted that. All we wanted to do was stop the pain."

But they had to operate, they said. He'd have died. But he's eighty-three, she said. That's when old men die. We have to take action, they said, as if her words were not important. He'd die, they explained, as if they had not heard.

They gathered around him, the brightest and best with their trays of scalpels and sutures. They broke open the cavern of his chest and worked in there in the blood and the shards of a torn blood vessel. They worked through drive-time and tea-time and prime-time, their feet comforted by clogs, their minds concentrated on the detail. They did it well, the team, and they did it fast. But it still took eleven hours and at the end of it a portion of the old man's bowel had died from lack of a blood supply. So they had to go on and do a colostomy also.

My mother saw him next in Intensive Care. A thick tube was taped fast to his face, rammed into his throat. I/Vs pumped clear liquids into him. Yellowed hoses drained fluids out of him into plastic bags taped at the side of the bed. Suction cups stuck to his chest and flexes ran over his shoulders, running to the machines that pulsated numbers in red and in neon green.

The high factory of Intensive Care made a noise of humming and beepings and metal clunking as sides of beds were put in place, all conducted by a thump-counting clock over the lit-up chest x-rays. Its red minute hand stuttered its way around and around the flat white face of it, while below the chests lined up, whitened with clouded toxicity.

My father swelled up, then swelled more, elegant hands fattened into massive childishness, his skin turned to sheeny fragility. They took him back into theatre to do more surgery. He came back and they began to train him for recovery the way you'd train an athlete into being a marathon runner. The great phrase was "Wean him off the ventilator." The power was reduced and the old man laboured, every tendon standing out, his nostrils sucked in by the effort, frail shoulders rising to drag up the chest and give space for the chalky lungs to expand. Scott sat with him after school, trying not to let his grandfather see how shockingly torturous he thought the therapy. Trying, also, to make friends on my father's behalf, with the ICU staff.

They shouted his Christian name at my father, and his eyes would widely open. The man everyone tended to call "Mr Clifford" now first-named intimately by white-garbed strangers. Through the mists, he could establish that some of these people with whom he was on unexpected first-name terms were black and one of them was male.

Whenever they put the ventilator back on full power, he would smile at them in sudden sweetness. In moments of negative activity – when he managed to pull out an I/V or a breathing tube – he would wink at them in triumph. Back would go the I/V. The tubes would work once more.

When they cut a hole in his throat and pushed a

ventilator tube directly into it, his mouth was free. Those of us who could lip-read got the drift of his thinking. "What's the point?" he would ask, repeatedly. No voice, but unmistakeable meaning.

When, in the night, they would briefly remove the throat tube to clean it, he could speak. Always the one sentence – "What's the point?" He wrote it on their pads, too. "What's the point?" Sometimes, because he could not see what he was writing, the questions ran together and overlapped in a tracing of wise bewilderment.

In the first days after the surgery, we were hushed and relieved. Relieved that he was not in pain and not appalled when they said he might not survive. Once conscious and on a respirator, he was a focus of different anxieties and confusions. They shouted at him that he was in great form and he looked at them with contempt. They reassured him when he had sought no reassurance. When he gestured towards the door and demanded to go home, they said he was confused. He could not argue with them, so he tried to demonstrate the reasons for his disbelief in their optimism, groping for the horror of the bags beneath the sheets until they tied his hands. Scott arrived at teatime one Tuesday to find my father asleep, his hands ribbon-tied to rails raised at the side of the bed. The boy put his forehead against the rail and cried silently. My father's hand, wetted by the teenager's tears, turned at the wrist to half-stroke the boy's face. My mother, who saw this, fought them for his freedom. They patiently explained that his confusion required that they restrain him.

"What confusion?"

"He wants to go home."

"But you're saying he's much better, so of course he's asking to go home. He wants to know when he can go home. Tell me and I'll tell him."

Well, of course, they said, you have to remember he's

in Intensive Care. There's his age. He was always a smoker, wasn't he?

"You're in there telling him he's great," she told them. "Tell me when he can go home."

It was, they said, too soon to know. This was after three weeks in the ICU cell, where he was bathed in a permanent daylight and treadmilled every hour by people whose faces he couldn't see.

"Twenty-two days of this and where's it got him to?"

They talked blood chemistry to her. Or tried to. The nurses (who didn't like her because she harped on missing things) were more honest. It was possible that he would recover enough to get out of Intensive Care. Possible. But if he did get out and into the main hospital, and if he eventually got out of the hospital, then he certainly couldn't go home. He would have to spend a year or so in rehab – some kind of nursing home.

She told them that was worse than death for him, and produced the document he had written. They told her it was irrelevant. She told them she would sue them.

"For what?" they asked.

"For operating before I signed a consent form."

"We could have gone ahead if you'd never signed it. We have to save lives."

"You didn't save his life. You prevented the death he was entitled to have. You took away all his rights."

They told her she hadn't a leg to stand on. His wishes were of no importance, she asked? That's not the issue, they said. She called them inhuman. They called her (to me and my brother) difficult.

"Of course she's difficult," Timothy told them furiously. "She's Our Lady of the Perpetually Shifting Premise. She argues and you end up so that you don't know whether it's Christmas or Tuesday. What's that got to do with it?"

It was important, they told him, not to take hope away

from the old man. The old man didn't have hope, Timothy said. Didn't like hope. Expected the worst from life, and by Jesus, didn't life deliver on his every expectation?

The old man had to have hope, they said implacably. Here was a man lying sleepless but with his eyes closed, day after day, hour after hour, bright night after bright night among strangers, ruled and regulated and weaned and driven towards a virtually impossible escape in the direction of another place of imprisonment. He had read us stories of heroes and gallants, of men unbroken by brainwashing because of their vision of where they would get to when they escaped, and we tied the hands that had held those books to a raised metal rail. Spavined him like an unthinking animal needing punishment.

Every day we went at different times and he would hear our voices and smile to us. We would take the tiny foam rubber lollipop stick and run it, wet, across his mouth. He would gesture for the pen and pad and write his message.

"What's the point?"

We would tell him there was a possibility of him coming off the respirator and he would hold out his hands. We unchained him, every time, and felt not heroes but traitors. He mimed the number of days he had been there, getting it right every time. Both hands outstretched four separate times meant forty days. Both hands stretched out five separate times meant fifty days. He begged us, on paper and in that silent speech of his, to let him go. To get him out. We explained the medical team's situation. He would lift up the hands and flutter the fingers upward at the door. Lest we mistake his message, he mouthed it without passion.

"Go home."

Go home, because you will not help me. Go home, because the false promise of your presence is harder to bear than your real absence. Go home because you *can* go home.

The gesture had an imperial flavour, ironic in someone so stripped of power.

We went home, and came back later. All of us, including Scott, who sat alone with him after rugby matches and murmured quiet things the rest of us will never know about. Scott walked long corridors away from the ICU and walked into a silence untypical of him before, but typical of him now. Timothy felt reproached by the quiet of his son and got more talkative and touchy.

My father lay in a bloodstained cell and on the fiftieth day, the blood was still on the walls, as if they had killed someone there and dragged him out thereafter. The cleaners came every day with spinning hoovers like those little dolls who used to twirl on mirrored musical boxes. It was a cotillion of cleanness, a dance only of duty.

In that bloodstained cell, the tortures were many and minuscule. There was no great breaking on a wheel, demanding facile once-off heroics. Instead, there were the medical people who called him Angus (like a bull) when his name was Aengus. They diagnosed him as depressed when he refused to answer. There was the sister who decided to give him a treat and soaked the foam-rubber lollipop in whiskey.

"Jesus, my father, when it comes to alcohol, makes Fr Matthew look like a wimp, you silly cow," Timothy told her when it was explained to him why my father had become so agitated, had dislodged his breathing tube and choked before they suctioned him back to exhausted ICU normality.

They put bronchoscopes down his tubes to get samples to send to the lab to figure out the identity of each bug which attacked him. They varied the antibiotics like Cecil B De Mille used extras. (This, again, Timothy's description.)

On the fifty-first day, there was no improvement. He laboured, his skin stretched across his shoulder blades, swellings huge, wounds unhealed. Nothing that had meaning to him was possible, other than the sweet smile with which he greeted us. When the hope of deliverance implied by our arrival receded, as it always did within minutes of our arrival, he would start to ask his question.

"What is the point?"

The pioneering young surgeon who had saved him from death could not accept that it would be proper, now, not to continue the fight.

"What he has now is not life," my mother said. "And what you're pushing him towards is not life either. If he was in a concentration camp in Central America and they were doing what you're doing to him, Amnesty International would be fighting to get them away from him."

"So you just want him dead?" the young surgeon asked, in a moment of cruelty. She wept in front of him, unable to tell him that my father, tied and tortured as he was, had developed a sweetness to her that she could only recollect from decades earlier. When their love had been hopeful and uncomplicated. (My father just asked the rest of us what was the point. He told her he loved her and that he was sorry. She told us this afterwards. She could not tell the surgeon.)

"Look, we're going to try growth hormone," the young surgeon said. "It's only experimental, but the signs are good."

She took her glasses off and palmed the tears away. Put the glasses back on and looked at him in silence.

"I hope you won't," she said eventually, and went back to the cell, where she held the old man through the network of tubes and wires as if she would protect him against the world. He slept. He worsened. The machine breathed him and he worsened.

The young surgeon stood in the door, silhouetted against the brighter outside.

"We'll leave him," he said simply. "We'll leave him be."

The Coming of Mrs Roper

It is almost two years now, and the ripples still have not reached out to the bank and died. His family were grimly unsurprised and mutely gleeful. My own people were baffled and bruised and very torn, because, you see, they liked him.

My mother will often, in mid-anecdote, amplify a tombstone description of someone I haven't met by saying "He's a lovely, big, generous man, like your Jim," and the realization will strike her in a tide of red and the rest of the sentence swallowed away.

I have told her that I like to hear Jim spoken well of, but she has never understood the separation, and assumes that there is an Awful Truth about Jim which I am keeping to myself out of shame.

I did tell anybody who wanted to know the reason why I left him, but, like an inept skin graft, it didn't take. People nodded and smiled and humoured me.

It reminded me of the plumber who reconstructed our bathroom. The house was an old one, with a queer old poky room at the top of the stairs, where lurked a bath which had been painted and allowed to peel, a toilet and a cracked washbasin, all jostling each other for space. If you stood up quickly from the loo, you cracked your skull off the medicine cabinet, and if you put down a bathmat, it would climb up the pedestal of the washbasin like one of those daft sums at school, where you're required to carpet the floor of a given room, and where a miscalculation means you end up with the room carpeted halfway to the ceiling. I decided that a shower and bidet combination would take up less space than the bath, and had all the existing hardware pulled out by Bah Corcoran. Bah was a friend of a friend and his real trade was bartending, but he did plumbing as a paying hobby. He was stout and talkative and quite disappointed when I waved away his coloured catalogues of avocado baths and plum loos.

"White everything," I said. "And I don't care what style. Just pick the ones that are easiest to plumb."

As it turned out, though, we had to use the catalogues anyway, to show him the bidet I wanted. He had never plumbed one before, nor registered its presence in the catalogues, being a man given to cursory glances rather than studious perusals, and so the difference between W/Cs and bidets had escaped him. I had my doubts about the possibilities of his actually returning with the required apparatus, since he pronounced it "B'dee", but the builders' providers obviously talked Bah's language, because three days later a bone-white bidet was delivered, along with toilet, handbasin and shower stall.

Every time I met him on the landing during the installing, he asked me the purpose of the B'dee. Every time, I would tell him the truth with brutal directness. Every time, he would laugh himself red in the face and bring on a coughing fit.

"Jaysus, Mrs G, you're a card," he would say, and return to the fray.

On the last day, he made protracted farewells, returning in *medias res* to the bidet.

"Tell us, Mrs G, tell us, joking apart, what that B'dee's for," he invited, toolbox under one arm.

For a second I contemplated dishing out the unacceptable truth again. And decided it would hurt him.

"I'll tell you, Bah," I said. "It's for soaking the baby's nappies in . . . "

That had the ring of truth about it, and he left happy. I have often wished, in the past two years, that there was a similarly neat and decent and acceptable lie that I might tell about Jim and me.

I have even made up a few. I thought of suggesting that he "made demands" on me, which non-specific demands, by implication, repelled me beyond coping. But I'd need to get it said quickly if it was to be believed at all. Another possible scenario I considered was the fiction that I had conceived a great and illegitimate passion for some other man, been ditched and am now living out days of retributive woe. Except that I am neither attractive enough to draw extramarital affections, nor energetic enough to act on any which might develop. I am fat and given to reading thrillers late at night, eating chocolate goldgrain biscuits.

I did, on Jim's beseeching, go with him to a marriage counsellor. It was not a success. Despite her best efforts (she was a sad-faced lady in good clothes with an eternity ring) she evidently decided that right was on Jim's side.

As I agreed with her, this put us in a logical impasse characterised on my part by a desire to laugh, and on hers by an overwrought effort to break through to a level of emotional significance which simply didn't exist.

Her gently probing questions were as silly and as persistent as the nightmare they provoked in me, where, for weeks on end, a quiet-spoken facsimile of the counsellor kept asking my sleeping self earnestly, "But could you tell me what the doughnut *meant?*"

Our friends had a worse problem. The marriage

counsellor had to deal only with Jim and me. To our friends, the composite picture of the disaster area included Micki, our four-year-old.

"But you *can't* leave Micki without a mother," they wailed, and names appeared like footnotes in their pleas – Bowlby, Spock, Jolly and Janov.

"But I'm not good at the basic mothering skills," I said, slipping into the jargon to show them that my defection was informed, not pig-ignorant. "In all of the important things like establishing routines for sleep and feeds and storytelling, Jim is much better than I am, and he does it with much more conviction. Micki sees through my efforts. And Jim *loves* being with Micki. One whole day with the child is too much for me".

They talked about custody and visiting days, and it took a long time to make it clear to them that Jim and I were going to live apart, but that neither of us wanted to take the other to court. I said I would have plenty of play-days with Micki, but after a while, I lost my audience. Unsatisfied with the basic story, superstructures were merely irritants to them.

The problem is, you see, that Jim and I are the perfect couple in almost every way.

And when the rot set in, it was a quiet, odd rot you'd never identify. I suppose I noticed it first in the car. Or rather, *not* in the car but at the kerb, where I would be standing, tail out to the rain, while he put last-minute findings of mine into my outstretched and cupped hand.

"Leave them," I'd say, unwilling to dissipate the lovely warmth of our evening together. "Leave them, sure I'll collect them in the morning."

"Ah, no, take them now," he'd say, handing me rolls of mints, pens and flat round containers of eyeshadow. Or, if I'd been to the newsagents, what he'd hand out would be the *Evening Herald*, half a Crunchie and an unopened cellophane bag of red pistachio nuts.

Later, he began to suggest that I pick up these articles before we got to our street, and for a time, I made a little joke of it, saying " . . . and please collect your personal belongings before you leave the aircraft."

Eventually, though, it spoiled the whole journey, as even one drop of bad milk will sour a cup of tea. From the moment I entered the car, I was waiting for it; that little exploratory glance of his around the dashboard nooks and crannies. It always happened just before we left the yellow lights of the main road for the white lights of suburbia.

Anticipation was the major problem, in the house, too. Anticipation of the moment when he would check the tines of his fork for grime before eating. Or the moment when I'd hear the characteristic sound of a plastic refuse sack being slapped open to provide a final resting place for my randomly dropped apple cores and sweet wrappings. I anticipated, too, his recurrent phrase as he investigated a pile of inappropriate objects, such, for example, as a pile of sheet music in the bedroom, or tinned fruit on the draining-board.

"Pet," he would begin, and my teeth would clench, Pavlov-dog fashion. "Pet, have you any particular reason for leaving these here?"

I would search for, or invent a reason. Or hesitate. And if I hesitated, he would lift the pile or whatever it was, and say, "Well, I'll just shift it, so. Give us more room."

Which it did, and I hated him for it. I loathed all the clean unobstructed surfaces he created around me. Their smooth gleaming planes struck a deep fear in me, like the repulsion modern Swedish furniture causes in me. Its simple functionality scares me. It will never do anything more or less, that's its job . . .

Then he got Mrs Roper. Someone recommended her to him, and he made out to me that he wanted to help her out, since the people who had recommended her had now gone to Canada.

"She used to do four hours a week for them," he said happily, "so I told her we'd take up the slack."

I protested, of course. I even cried, saying that he must hate his home and the way I kept it, but he was, surprisingly, unmoved.

"Listen, Pet," he said in a sensible voice. "That's all very silly. Not only do you have the child on your hands, you work as well . . . "

"Part-time teaching," I said. "Doesn't exactly tie me hand and foot."

"Nevertheless," he said. "You shouldn't have to do all the housework as well. Having Mrs Roper will free you to do more of the things around the house that you like doing – cooking, for instance."

I joked uneasily about him now expecting gourmet food all the time, but he was already sorting out in his mind where Mrs Roper would start.

She started, predictably enough, in the kitchen, whose spectacular disorder she took in with one grimly unsurprised glance. The first day she found a dirty nappy down the back of the washing-machine, and saved it, along with other long-lost odds and ends to proffer at the end of her four hours. She asked me would I be needing the nappy. I threw it into the rubbish container, trying to make a laugh of the whole thing. I had little choice. The baby had been toilet trained a full year by then.

It was all right when she was a muffled banging presence in the kitchen. Upstairs, I could almost forget about her. Jim, on the other hand, wanted her to make progress.

"Is Mrs Roper out of the kitchen yet?" he would ask. "Has she started the dining-room yet?"

Soon she did, and the relentless march of the clean

shiny surfaces continued. In the kitchen, sun struck the formica with such reflective power that you'd get snow-blindness from it. The other rooms began to look as if they belonged in a show house. She began to work her way up the paintwork alongside the stairs with a terrible gaunt energy, and I felt as the passengers on the Titanic deck must have felt as the lower reaches of the stricken ship filled with water to a higher and higher level.

In addition to the sense of impending doom, the truth was borne in on me that I had not created the shambles we lived in through overwork or error.

I had done it with unknowing intent. Like the two old brothers in America who never threw out newspapers, but piled them up, decade on decade, in increasingly complex mazes until one of the paper piles gave way, and cut them off from food and help. I needed my womb of dirt and clutter. Inside it, I felt toasty and secure.

So, the day Mrs Roper reached our bedroom door, I left and moved in here. It's not much. One room, basically, with a little alcove for sink and cooking, but it's cheap. That's important, because of course Jim shouldn't have to contribute – or be at financial loss. I made that clear to him, even if I left him pretty fogged about everything else. Nor did I take many things from the house. Only those possessions I had before we got married. Or some of them.

That's the other good thing about this bedsit. It's small enough. Even my few belongings make a mess of it.

THE DIGNY MADONNA

IVOR WAS ICILY SOBER AND THINKING OF GOING HOME WHEN HE saw her for the first time. She was one of a group around Mick Geraghty, who was doing impressions. The others in the group were laughing and lurching about, pushing each other to indicate how funny Geraghty was being. The girl was standing, a half-smile on her broad, pale face, hands hanging loosely at her sides.

Ivor delighted in the simplicity of the stance. He looked around him. People leaning on the backs of chairs, or mantlepieces, drinks in hand. Nobody but the pale girl standing straightly, unaffectedly, like a school-girl awaiting instructions. He nudged Rafferty.

"Who's your one beside Geraghty?"

"Who?"

"The one with the dark hair."

Rafferty gave him an ostentatiously knowing look. Her hair was her least noticeable feature.

"Ciúnas Digny," Rafferty said.

A silence fell, thick and dispiriting.

"So?" said Ivor.

"So she's an alcoholic and a messer."

"Are we talking about the same one?"

"The white dress with the rope thing around the middle," Rafferty said flatly.

"But Jesus, she's only about twenty-two, twenty-three."

"Less. She's the eldest of Claude Digny's lot."

Ivor made what he hoped was a noncommittal noise.

"You shouldn't have come off the jar," Rafferty said sourly. "You'd more sense with a few in."

The girl, Ivor realised, when he got close to her, was drunk. Quietly, grimly, consumedly, drunk. She was also more beautiful at close range, in a dated way, like an old painting; almost heavy, her skin thick, creamy and, despite the heat of the room, even in tone. She accepted his presence and his self-introduction with a massive calm, giving her own name as something recently learned by rote.

Geraghty was winding to a halt, and Ivor found it easy to steer the dark girl into a corner.

He talked a great deal, nervously, and she listened. When he paused, she spoke with an air of isolating the most important point for development.

"You're not drinking."

"No," he said, put off his stroke by the *non sequitur.*

"You haven't had anything to drink."

The words were not slurred, but articulated with the great care of the very drunk. It sounded as if her tongue was a large damp sponge.

"No."

"Why?"

"I haven't been drinking for three weeks."

"Why?"

No wasted new inflection. The repeated question fell without melody, like a tired drumbeat.

"You don't want to know that," he said, trying to change conversational gear. "The thing is – "

"Why?"

"I thought I was dangerously near becoming an alcoholic, so I stopped."

There was a pause. Then she put her hand on his sleeve, part-caress, part-support and that was the end of the conversation. He went home, stunned and puzzled and slept badly.

When, ten days later, the phone rang and he called her by her name after her first words, she seemed neither surprised nor flattered.

"Can I come and stay with you?"

Ivor uttered a clutch of wavering half-sentences, baffled by the directness of the request. He almost said "But I hardly know you." She waited until the sounds died away, and waited again. He looked at himself in the hall mirror.

His face was blotchy and it shone. Christ, he thought, the best offer you're ever likely to have and you're bloody near turning it down because she hasn't hedged it around sufficiently.

"Yes, of course," he said.

She arrived within twenty minutes, carrying a single battered suitcase with brown toe-caps on each corner.

He thought her thin coat inadequate for the February cold, but she looked just as she had at the party, except more tired. She was sober, too.

He made her coffee, avoiding her eyes during the preparation, maintaining the civil pretence that she didn't quite exist until a sketchy meal enabled each to acknowledge the other and talk. As he watched her covertly, he became aware that this process was alien to her. Her silence was not a preparation or a ploy. It was a physical trait, like the creamy skin. She sat with a repose he had never seen before in a woman, looking around his room with trance-like incuriosity. He waited for her to notice the long wall, covered floor to ceiling in loaded bookshelves. Women, in his experience, responded either with wide-eyed admiration – 'Have you actually *read* all these books?' – or with a flinty inquisitiveness which drew them close to the titles for examination. Ciúnas looked at the bookshelves as though they were devoid of any significance; with the unresponsive openness of a pre-literate savage. As if the book-backs were merely a differently textured wall, not units of pleasure or learning.

The kettle boiled and he poured scalding water onto powder in two mugs. She took one, held it between her palms, and lowered her face to it woodenly. As the hot liquid met her tongue, her whole mouth twisted violently, and a convulsive dry retching overtook her. Automatically, he clapped a hand to her forehead and held her.

"I'm sorry," she said. "I should have told you that might happen."

"How long is it since you had a drink?"

"Thirteen hours."

"Are you thirsty?"

A nod. He went to the kitchen and mixed Coca-Cola with the recently boiled water. The taste made her shudder, but the retching was not repeated. Eventually, she set the glass down and looked at him. God, he thought, she's waiting for questions. The inevitability of catechism.

"That night of the party, I had just discharged myself from St Lomans," she said. "I didn't want to be there any more. I thought I would just not drink. But it didn't work out."

She made it sound as ungovernable as weather.

"So I remembered you and you saying you were off it and I thought I'd come here."

The rounded arrogance of her assumption of welcome pleased something in Ivor long concealed from himself. With barely controlled glee, he showed her the bedroom, unpacked her unrelated bits and pieces (she evinced no interest in unpacking) gave her a mild sleeping pill and put her to bed. All afternoon, he watched her. She slept like someone in an ad for sheets, he decided; gracefully, one hand tucked under her cheek. When she woke, it was with a huge and merry smile. This, he later discovered, was an integral part of her. No matter how ill or hungover she was, the first awakening always included this total, rollicking smile, which gradually faded into undisappointed acceptance as the day wore on.

For weeks after her arrival she could eat nothing but baby foods. He had the habit of feeding her himself since her interest would wane and the spoon slow to a halt if he left her to feed herself. Nobody looked for her. She never answered his phone. For a time, when he answered, he expected to hear an anxious enquiry about her but none came.

"Who'd want to know where I am?" This from her, when he commented.

"Well, your family. A boyfriend."

"My family will be glad I'm not messing them up," she said. "And you're my boyfriend."

He was quite ridiculously pleased by this guileless validation.

"Are you upset about your family?"

"About my family what?"

"Not wanting – being glad you're not around."

"No."

End of story, he murmured. Her monosyllables fell softly and deadeningly onto his worries. He often felt he was like a parrot submerged into silence by a blanket carelessly thrown over the cage. He quite enjoyed the sensation. It was like a licensed return to childhood, this freedom from worry. He had for many years carried the weight of an acquired solemnity.

There was a daily challenge to him to amuse and

entertain her, to draw a response from that calm preoccupied face.

When she casually admired a flowering cherry tree, he bought one and had it planted in the tiny garden of the little town house. When she sickened of baby food, he took her to the best restaurant he knew. The waiter served them from a semi-crouch, trying to meet Ciúnas' eye and make her smile. Ivor chose the food. She ate little.

"Do you not like it?"

"Oh, it's good," she said. "You shouldn't waste your money on food like this for me. I was brought up on ice cream and chips."

He laughed, thinking it a joke. Later, chance comments filled in the truth of it. The Digny marriage had brought together the most celebrated painter of his day and the most striking artist's model of her's, into a relationship fraught with jealousies, infidelities, children (eight of them) pitched battles and alcohol. Ciúnas was the first of the eight. Ivor ached with sympathy for her, a sympathy bottled into pointless bile by her lack of sentimentality. Whatever self-pity she owned had long been transmuted into a boundless capacity for alcohol.

Occasionally, Ivor would describe their relationship to a colleague as one of friendship. Invariably he met with an incredulous stare. The Digny Madonna did not move in with you out of friendship. Ivor blinked and resigned himself to possession of a small unacceptable truth: he lacked Ciúnas' ability to make her simple truthfulness into a social tool.

Once, at a party, he watched her while someone told a series of elephantine sex jokes. Someone asked her reaction.

"I don't understand," she said, and everyone laughed.

The Digny Madonna knew more than she was letting on, said the looks and the laughter. Ivor Marrinan was the bright spark to have got hold of her when he did.

Most of the time, he would have agreed. Not a handsome or witty man, he was pleased to stand aside and watch her effect on others, how the splendid positive shape of her attracted attention and her grave silences drew conversation from people as salt draws spilled wine from a tablecloth. He would probe to find out what went through her head when the velvety silences fell. She was never secretive.

"I was trying to remember if water boils quicker if you stir it or if you leave it alone."

He would embark on an explanation, only to see the small curiosity ebb away from her eyes.

"It's all right," she would say. "I don't *mind* not knowing. I was just thinking."

She was greatly absorbed by day to day minutiae and would spend half an hour painstakingly peeling away the membrane from the empty shell of a hard-boiled egg. Nor was she stupid. She would listen, and then, whatever the topic, make a single comment which often silenced him by its perception. When he brought friends to the little house, her judgements on them often crystallised his own shapeless views.

"I don't like that Rafferty," she said one day. "He smells like a funeral."

By then, Ivor had given up trying to analyse her occasional pronouncements. Rafferty, he agreed, did smell like a funeral.

Occasionally, and only in bed, she would do uncannily accurate impersonations of friends of his, and he would laugh until tears ran into the wrinkles at the side of his eyes, and hold her.

Twice in six months, she drank. At their first party, she silently abandoned her tomato juice and drank brandy with suicidal concentration. Afterwards, she was sick for almost a week. In August, after a visit to her mother, she disappeared for four days and announced her return by breaking Ivor's two front windows. Unlike alcoholics he had known, she suffered neither guilt nor remorse, but took up her life after a binge with grace and sureness. Nor, following the second episode, did she seem to remember pawning two pieces of jewellery he had given her. He found the pawn tickets in a pocket and redeemed the brooch and ring.

The second binge was known about. Rafferty was quick to offer gloating sympathy.

"I did warn you what sort she is," he told Ivor.

"You don't *know* what sort she is," Ivor snapped, and afterwards repeated it to himself with private satisfaction.

Towards Christmas, he was in the grip of an excitement he had not felt for twenty years. He bought particularly pretty gift paper in October and ribbon to match. He constantly window-shopped for her. Buying a tree became part of his Christmas plan although he had never had one in the house before. He decided, too, to give her money. Normally, they shopped together and he paid. Or he collected eggs and bread and brought them home.

"There's no point in giving me money," she had told him. "I never 'just buy' anything. Ever. Except drink."

Now he broached the subject with diffidence.

"I'm sure you want to give presents to your family."

"No?" she said, surprised.

"Well, to the younger children," he pursued, willing her to show a streak of sentiment.

"If you want me to," she said in friendly acquiescence and sank into reverie.

"Penny for them?"

"What? No, I was just thinking how you want me to be involved with my family."

"Well, families are important."

"Oh? Oh, yes. I suppose so."

He dropped her in town early on the Tuesday morning before Christmas. The queue of parents and children for Switzers Santa was already turning the corner into Wicklow Street. She had a list he had made out of people to be bought for. She wore a new winter coat he had given her, her pale face framed in soft fur. At the last moment, when he was pulling the car out into the traffic, she rapped on the passenger window. He leaned over and rolled it down.

"I never said thank you," she said and smiled her early morning smile.

By lunchtime, he had the tree standing, wedged in an aluminium bucket. And decorated. He had bought ten boxes of ornaments. That done, he wrapped several gifts for her in different kinds of paper and arranged them beneath the tree. It looked, he thought, a real family tree. Then he made sandwiches, and put on records, stacking them on his old-fashioned record player like aircraft waiting to land. One following another, they softly fell and the needle dropped.

When the pile was spent he turned the lot over and they peeled off the half-hours until ten o'clock. He rebuilt the fire, took the presents from beneath the tree and stashed them in the back of a wardrobe. No point in rubbing it in, he thought, and sat down to wait. At half past three he got into his car and slowly drove around the city, trying to suppress a bitter little thought that even if he saw her, he wouldn't recognise her quickly in the new coat. Always assuming she still had the new coat . . .

At dawn, he went home. The alternating circuits made the tree lights wink at him with hiccuping gaiety. He kicked the plug loose and went to bed.

During the next four days he became obsessed by a determination not to cancel the turkey. Cancelling the turkey assumed the treacherous haste of Moses striking the

rock twice. If he didn't do it all would be well. At four
o'clock on Christmas Eve he went, shamefaced, to the
butcher who told him not to worry, he had plenty of takers
for a ten pound hen. Relinquishing the turkey was a final
thing, like letting go the string of a kite. He went home,
took three books, a packet of biscuits, a lump of cheese
and a bottle of milk, and went to bed for Christmas.

The day after Stephen's Day a call came from Vincent's
Hospital. Was he? Yes. He was. Why? Well, they had this
young woman who'd been admitted from Casualty on
Stephen's Day and his name was in her handbag. On a
scrap of paper. Misery clogged his voice as he reflected
that the piece of paper was undoubtedly there since her
first call in February. The cool social worker voice paused.
He would come over? Good.

He brought her clothes in the battered suitcase, and her
presents on top as an afterthought. (He took the wrapping
off and left them in their boxes and tissue paper). When he
reached the hospital he asked the social worker first how
long they were likely to keep her in.

"I can't tell you that, Mr Marrinan, she's very ill, you
know."

No, he didn't know.

She wasn't supposed to discuss medical matters, but . . .
But?

"I do know that apart from her . . . illness, she's had a
fall. And she's in an oxygen tent."

"Pneumonia?"

She shrugged agreement.

"So she could be here a month. Or more. Right?"

She looked blank, puzzled by his insistence.

"I want to pay you for six weeks now. OK?"

No. She had no idea what charges there would be. Or
how long –

"Then I suggest you make a bloody good guess," he

said, slapping his cheque book down on an onyx table. "Because what I don't pay you right now, you're never going to get."

He was ferociously, unreasonably angry. The girl clucked and wavered. Eventually she named a sum with the terrified recklessness of someone at an auction for the first time. Hedged it around with comments about cheques not committing anyone to anything.

He wrote the cheque and filled the stub with all of the details.

"You'll want to see her," the girl said, holding the cheque like an admission ticket.

"No. I won't," he said, numb with the decision.

Well, would they let him know about her progress? No. Thank you. No.

Would she put his address down as her home? No. He gave her Claude Digny's address, right down to the district number. She thanked him curtly and left, the cheque dangling from her hand.

Ivor went slowly down the stairs, his mind puzzling over the oddly empty feeling of his hands. After some thought he identified what was missing. The suitcase he had carried upstairs.

He pulled gloves out of his coat pocket and made himself busy putting them on.

PLATO'S APOLOGY

I'M NOT PUSHED, REALLY. I'LL HAPPILY DO BAGGING AT THE BACK of the shop, drag the filmy plastic down over the dresses and smack the hot metal A-frame into place so it melts tear-off perforated lines above the shoulders.

Bagging lets you set your own pace. There are days when you'll be in great form and you'll lash those clean, flattened garments up on to the moving conveyor faster than you ever thought you could. Then there are days when you lounge along, singing with the pressers, their voices rising through the steam and the chemical smells and the thumping of the irons.

My favourite position, though, is tag-and-toss. Tag-and-toss is where you take the clothes over the counter from the customers, tag each item, and toss it into one of the great wheeled bag-trolleys behind the swing curtain.

When you're on tag-and-toss you get to put faces on the owners of the clothes. It becomes as interesting as a doctor's surgery. We had one customer whose teenager daughter was a bit dippy. She'd spend three months in a mental hospital, come out with all her thinking processes bright and fast as a colour print, and then gradually, over the ensuing year, they would fade into dysfunctionality.

That's another thing. You pick up the language of the customers. Bart, at the back of the shop, used to notice me doing it.

"Dysfunctional," he would repeat, after I'd told a story about a customer. "*Dysfunctional?* What the hell does that mean? That your one is gone off the deep end again? Loopy? Half-mad? Not to fart around about it, she's daft as a frigging brush?"

You would always know when the dysfunctional daughter was back in the hospital because her mother would arrive with armloads of her clothes. It wasn't just that they were dirty, although they were so dirty it was obvious she had worn some garments for weeks on end. She used to attack them, too. Slash the sleeves with a razor blade right through to her own skin, so that there was always a debate in the back of the shop as to whether the blood should be got out first, or the neat slashes mended before the stain specialist went to work on the darkened stiffness of blood shed and absorbed a month previously.

Then there was the youngish man who one day brought in a complete baby's layette. Everything from velvety hand-knitted cardigans with tiny pearl buttons, to lambs-wool decorative cot-blankets. I turned them and tagged them, pinning miniature booties together so they wouldn't be lost in the big drum.

"No special stains that I'm missing?" I asked, because the whole lot seemed very clean. Just a faint scent of baby powder.

The man was watching what I was doing with a rigid fascination and for a moment didn't seem to hear me. Then the words came out of him in that hate-filled monotone people learn when they need to contain a distended misery.

"Giving them away," he said. "My son died. SIDS."

SIDS? Oh, yes, SIDS. Cot death. In silence I handed him the twenty tags, concertinaed for his wallet. He gave me a blinking nod to acknowledge his realisation that I wasn't being uncaring; that I realised his grief was unreachable by the kindness of strangers. Whenever he came back after that we talked about the weather or about something in that morning's newspaper.

On the other hand there are times when you see people arriving with an armful of clothes and the reasons are not sad. They're just back from holiday, or they're spring-cleaning. Or they've lost weight so they're ready to wear their "thin" clothes again.

When the Perfessor brought in her two black plastic sacks of clothes, I assumed at first that she was heading off to lecture in some other country. She dumped them and said she'd come back for the tags later that day, as she sometimes did when she was in a hurry. When she wasn't in a hurry she would ask me what I was reading, because she had noticed that whenever I was on tag-and-toss at the front of the shop and there wasn't much happening, I would be reading.

"How do you pick what you read?" she asked one afternoon when the yellowed paperback I upended, open page side down on the counter, turned out to be *The Brothers Karamazov.*

"Has to be second-hand, for starters," I said, my speech slightly sibilant as I talked through pins held in my teeth. "For cheapness."

I didn't tell her that I like the smell of second-hand books, that sweetly stale tea-caddy scent of ageing poor-quality paper. Nor that I like the evidence of deterioration; the page-corners forming broken arches instead of sharply-angled corners, as if they'd been gently nibbled.

"Then, if I discover an author I like, I try to get anything that author's written. So I've gone through phases of Hemingway or Kotzwinkle or Updike. I'm always way out of date."

She laughed and was gone. Thereafter, she would note the book and ask about it. Most of them she knew.

"Well, she would, wouldn't she?" was Bart's comment. "Shagging Perfesser, she is."

"Of what?"

"Don't know. You ask her, since you're so pally with her."

When I did, she looked hunted and said she wasn't a professor, only a lecturer. In some aspect of literature. But she was more eager to ask me if a silk blouse she had been given at Christmas should be dry-cleaned at all.

"Absolutely not," I said, shoving the bundle of soft vividness back across the counter to her. "Warm water and Quix. Much better for it."

She noticed my fingers automatically fondling the texture of the fabric.

"You don't ever wear silk," she said and then looked surprised at having said it.

"Couldn't stand the thought of all the worms in the teacups," I said. She looked at me blankly.

"D'you not know how silk was discovered?"

The dry fizzy rusty hair piled untidily on her crown wobbled as she shook her head.

"Oh, some Chinese empress was out in her garden six million years ago, and a silkworm blew off a tree and fell in her teacup. The heat of the tea killed it, and its cocoon immediately started to unwind and reveal itself as this wonderful soft strong yarn. So she had it woven, and then began boiling the bejasus out of every silkworm she could find. I think it's lovely stuff, but it'd give me the creeps to think about boiling worms."

She stuffed the blouse into her handbag in a parody of shame and went off, shaking her head.

The day that she brought in the two big black sacks of clothes, I left the tagging to another girl because Bart was in full voice that afternoon, and I wanted to sing with him in the back of the shop. Bart has a powerful beautiful voice and he owns every record ever made by Nicolai Gedda. Sometimes, in the afternoons, this barrel-chested hard-drinking master of profanity lifts a melody on the power of a voice trained only by imitation, and sings great arias without any understanding of the words he has learned. I harmonise. When Bart left at four that evening, the whomping of the machines and the clanking of the conveyor seemed like percussion devoid of melody. I continued to sing on my own.

I have perfect pitch and the knack of imitating almost any singer you care to name. Just as some people can do a take-off of any politician, once they've heard them speak once or twice, I can do a singing take-off of any female soloist. That afternoon I was doing the old track from that bleached blonde singer who used to be with the Eurythmics: 'Angel Playing with my Heart'. I love the risky runs the voice takes in that song. The girl on tag-and-toss had taken a lift with Bart and skived off a bit early and I could hear the front doorbell going, indicating that a customer had arrived. As I walked through the curtain of divided plastic slats, I was trailing off the end of the song.

The Perfesser was there, looking very startled.

"You've a lovely voice."

I shrugged.

"I need to take on someone else's style before my voice exists. I know you've come back for the tags, but in fact we got through all your stuff this afternoon. So if you want, you can take them all with you now?"

"Oh, excellent," she said and went to lock her car door.

When she came back I already had a fair few of the garments, plastic-bagged and gathered into a big yellow carrier and was starting on the next lot.

"You moving house?" I asked.

"I am starting a complete new life," she said, as if she was beginning a speech, and went on to tell me that she'd got a legal separation from her husband, her two teenage children were going to spend most of their time with him (this delivered with a thrust of the chin, as if to dare me to make a negative judgement against her based on the proffered fact) and she was moving to an artisan's cottage in the Liberties to start all over.

"I gave all my old clothes to the VdeP and brought all my better stuff here and there you have it."

I stood still for a moment, then went to the yellow bag I had already sealed. While she watched I unsealed it and pulled out the clean garments.

"Is this your better stuff?"

On top was a man's jumper covered in fabric pills and darned at the elbows.

"Oh sweet Jesus."

She burrowed underneath the jumper and came upon garment after garment. Each past its best, but each, because of Bart's expertise, sadly clean and earnestly smooth. They looked thin and defeated.

"Oh, sweet *Jesus.*"

"You gave your good stuff to the Vincent de Paul, right?"

An affirmative nod.

"Could you get back to them quickly and say you made a mistake?"

"Christ I couldn't. I couldn't go to them and say 'look, I wanted to give you rubbish, but I gave you good stuff instead, give it back.' *I couldn't.*"

I said nothing. She looked at the clothes as if she could will them into changing into what they were supposed to be. Then looked at me. And I laughed.

It wasn't just that I laughed. Laughter squirted right through me and came burbling out of my mouth, of my eyes. Laughter entangled my breathing. It watered my eyes and filled my ears and there was nothing I could do about it. After a few seconds, it took her over too and the stiff thin shoulders jiggled as the pallid face crinkled with the spasms of it. Tears squeezed out of the sides of her eyes.

Eventually, it left us one on either side of the counter, each caught by the occasional haphazard snort of an indrawn breath catching on leftover laughter as a sleeping child gives an unexpected sob catching on leftover tears.

"Feck the whole lot in your dustbin," she said, holding out two twenty-pound notes. I dealt with the bill and gave the change. Just as she was going, she touched my forearm, bright in taut Lycra.

"Thank you," she said and was gone.

It was that day I fell in love with her.

It was that day she fell in love with me.

The choice was made before the justification presented itself. That happens a lot in my life. Maybe in everybody's life. I opt for something on instinct and then scrabble for acceptable reasons.

It was enjoyable, the weeks during which the signs and symptoms of loving her grew. The sensuality of a love affair is most subtle and vivid before the senses are consciously engaged. She would come into the shop and I would register the way she seemed to have been hung, damp, from the shoulders. Or her smoke-seamed face which made her look older than she was. When I went through the plastic slats into the back of the shop I could feel her watching me. Even when she arrived on my days off, I would enjoy the stomach-dropping wallop when Bart would say "The Perfesser was in yesterday. Didn't leave us sackfuls of castoffs this time. Didn't ask for you, either."

For me, it was easy and sequential as opening a can of soft drink, with the same incremental rewards. The negative reward of no fingernail breakage when the can opened cleanly. The spurt of compressed air. The first mouthfuls, acerbic in their aggressive aeration. Then the slightly flatter taste of the rest. Upending the can and teasing out the last drops before crushing the can as flat as any man could crush it, with the noise and tearing of the thin aluminium.

For her, I learned, no event – not even falling in love – could happen without an explanatory context. Her every step was cautioned by envisaged complications. Even asking me to dinner. When she did it, the request, from rehearsal, was shiny as a much-handled plum.

"Where?" I asked.

"In my home?"

It should have been a statement, but became a question through fear of offence. Maybe, her expression said, maybe you think that I think that you're not sophisticated enough to take to a classy restaurant.

"Oh, your home would be great," I said. "I'm not sophisticated enough to take to a classy restaurant."

She disavowed the thought with such vehemence it was obvious to both of us that it had been precisely what she was thinking.

"And furthermore," I said. "Don't waste your time doing quails in aspic or something like that. I live on kebabs, curries and crisps."

She found even that enthralling, because she was in the brain-dead stage of infatuation. As I found when I went to dinner. The very fact that I wore much the same kind of clothes as I wore in the dry-cleaning shop captivated her as evidence of a natural social sure-footedness.

"But I don't *have* cocktail dresses and things like that," I said. "When I've paid for my flat, for food, for the odd trip to the cinema and for books, I have frig all left, and nowhere to wear it anyway."

She had her hands in the sink, washing off a saucepan,

when she realised that her sleeves weren't pushed up far enough and turned to me, hands out, palm to me. Ridged white in counterpoint to the slightly raised veins of her wrist. I touched the ridges and looked a question. When it went unanswered, I rolled the sleeves back and she finished washing the pot.

"You obviously didn't read up on methods before you tried it."

"*Methods?*"

"Well, you didn't do it right. Doing it cross-ways is ineffective. You have to do it long-ways. Plus, it's one of the least efficient methods, because it's painful. Sleeping pills are the best. Painkillers are dodgy. If you do it with paracetamol and don't get it right, you make ribbons out of your kidneys and you're never the same afterwards."

"How do you know?"

"Just curious," I said, obeying her gesture and sitting down to eat. The starter included a lot of that funny lettuce that's like tangled green hair.

"Curious?"

"Yes. Whenever I come across something interesting I read up about it. One of my customers had a husband – "

For a moment I hesitated. Maybe the things people told you in a dry-cleaners came under a referred seal of the confessional. No, I decided. Anyway, I wouldn't name the customer.

"She had a husband who couldn't do it unless he had frilly knickers on. She really didn't care if he needed cowboy boots hanging from each ear, as long as he got on with it and didn't make a shagging supreme court case out of it, but he got very – " I fished for a word and tried to get the curly lettuce onto a fork.

"Conflicted?"

"Right. So he drank Paraquat. He survived it, but every time he got a cold after that, he ended up in hospital with pneumonia. She'd bring in all his suits whenever he was in hospital, that's how I found out about it. So I read up all about suicide."

She cleared away the plates.

"Suicide is very interesting," I added. "Did you know that people who commit murder are more likely to try to commit suicide when they're in jail than people in jail for a non-violent crime?"

There was no answer, and when I turned round to look at her, she was watching me with a mixture of amusement and delight. I knew why: anybody else who had seen her scars had offered support, concern or counselling. I knew to touch her and silence her and make love to her. And I did.

My ease discomfited her. She needed our affair to be an epiphany. (She had to explain that one to me. Any epiphany, as far as I was concerned, had to have three Kings on camels.) As did her friends. They were glad for her. But glad in a way reeking of dammed-up commiseration.

"Have you met George?" they would ask me, the question heavily undertoned.

"No," I would say.

Baulked of the permission of a question, they would leak sighs indicative of wife-battery, perversion, verbal abuse and Other Younger Women.

"Does Jessica not tell you about him?"

"No."

Eventually, one of them – another academic – came to the point.

"Have you *no* interest in her life before you met her?"

"Not yet. I haven't finished being interested in her life right now."

The eyes became slatey.

"Wonderful child," the friend said to Jessie.

"She means I'm a toyboy or the female equivalent," I

told Jessie that night in bed. Jessie was edgy. She wanted to turn out the light because the narrow neon strips built into the bookshelves over the head of the bed sucked any colour out of her face and aged her. She never understood that I found the signs of age delightful. I loved the softly crumpled paper-like texture of the skin below her collar bones. The fragility of her breasts I thought more interesting to touch than the almost muscular firmness of my own.

"That doesn't bother you because you're young," Jessie said.

"No. It doesn't bother me because I live now. All your pals either live in the past or live in their plans for the future. Either they want to talk about the shagging contraceptive train or about the perfect world they're going to create. I just like *now*."

"You are teaching me how to live," she said in the dark after I turned out the light.

That night she stopped loving me.

The choice was made before the justification presented itself. It was oddly enjoyable, in the following weeks, to watch the accretion of the signs and symptoms. I had not realised, up to then, that the traits that make us love someone are the traits that validate us in later loathing them.

My misuse of words had tickled her and struck her as creative and insightful. In these weeks there was less laughter, more immediate correction. Jealous wasn't the same as envious, she told me. Disinterested wasn't the same as uninterested, she explained.

She took less relish in my absorption in trivia. Earlier, if she came upon me rapt in delight watching a perfect jet trail being chalked across a sunny sky, she would slide her arms around my waist and watch it, as if she could suck an extra pleasure from it by being physically in touch with me. Now, she registered trivia as trivia and when, one night, she noticed me paring to sharpness every pencil in the house and sniffing the fresh parings for the woody smell, she looked repelled, as if the action was marginally nauseating. A habit of holding hot liquids in my mouth, trapped between tongue and roof of mouth, became so irritating to her that I began to avoid drinking tea in her presence.

Acknowledge what was happening to her, she would not. The gatherings of her friends continued and she always wanted me to be there, even though I never knew the names of the people they talked about and hated the guilt-free way they bitched.

"You *know* how wonderful I think Elaine is," they would stay. "There is simply *nobody* with a better insight into . . . "

You could count in your head and before you reached ten they had reached the kicker:

" . . . but in *this* instance, I have to say . . . "

Wham, Bam. Elaine, you're gone for your chips.

They needed enemies and crises and causes. Because I didn't need any of those things they found me shallow, trivial and unmannerly.

Early on they called me delightful. Later they found me 'amusing'. When they call you amusing you're done for. Amusing is for wine. Amusing is for furniture that's somewhere between innovative and tacky. In the beginning they had all swung in behind Jessie's discovery of me as a joyful natural. Baby Grandma Moses. Later, in unconscious response to her own changing view of me, they found me ripe for improvement. They first loved my random references, then decided I had a magpie mind. But they didn't hold it against me. It was a flaw for which I was not responsible. That was the kind of flaw they really liked. Anything that qualified another woman for generous rescue by them was a good thing. One of them had spent a year as a researcher on the *Late Late Show*, and she thought Gay Byrne was ripe for improvement too – and in much the same way.

"He's really bright," she assured them. "You'd have no idea. Really bright. I kept telling him he should do a degree. He'd be well able to. Like yourself he's a great reader but it's not systematic."

I nodded appreciatively and went off to refill platters in the kitchen. In no hurry to go back, I boiled a cup of water in the microwave and made a cup of instant coffee. (I prefer it to real coffee.) A few weeks earlier, I had stuck a photograph of the two of us up on the little corkboard and now I noticed Jessie had put a telephone list half over it. Obscuring her, not me. Because the photograph made her feel old.

"The generation gap," she had said tetchily.

The two miniature figures were in sharp contrast. She, slender to emaciation, all angles and washed-sand colours. Me, shorter and not fat, but more substantial, in neon pinks and lime greens. Like many a jury, the picture came to the wrong verdict.

From the other room, I could hear them disassembling my happiness in their need to fit it into a significance it didn't want, in their generational need to add meaning and values to the randomness of real life. People who are unhappy always want to improve the lives of people who are happy. When I went back in, a platter in each hand, they had me neatly sited somewhere between project and victim, ready for re-design. I ate Hula Hoops in smiling, passive resistance. Eventually, one of them gave up, with a backward swipe.

"I envy you," she lied. "The unexamined life . . . "

As she said it, she brought her two hands up to shoulder level to sketch quote marks around the spoken phrase. My own arm went out in stiff-armed Nazi salute and the gesture wrote *finis* to everything. The choice had already been made by Jessie – a choice for solidarity with the sisters – but the consternation of that night made her cruel in her speed. Or maybe not so cruel.

It is the sharpness and the speed of the Halal beef-killer's knife that makes the execution both efficient and painless. It was like that. Within a week, I had a flat of my own. Within three, Bart had noticed her absence.

"The Perfesser move away?"

"I think so."

Nobody else at work noticed. I felt no great impulse to leave and start afresh. No hunger for epiphanies.

About Week Four, a woman brought in a bundle of clothes she had taken out of the house where her parents had lived. She carried them in an old suitcase with a black belt around it. She was in a hurry so I said I'd sort them and hold the suitcase for her. I noticed that something had been stuffed into the bottom of the case. I pulled it out, it was a copy of an old comic called *Judy*, from six years before I was born. I opened it up and all the characters were girls who were skating or horse-riding or jumping on pogo sticks. There was one story about a girl who played a trombone. At the bottom of the two pages taken up by each episode of another serial was a line like "*Look out for next week's episode of SpeedSkater Sue*". That's it, I thought. Look out for next week's episode of the Unexamined Life.

I saved the comic for the customer. You never know, it might be valuable. We have a special drawer for the things we find in pockets, so I put it in there.

DIES IRAE

THEY MET AT THE DOOR OF THE OLD HOUSE AT HALF PAST TWO.
Sisters, neat in not-quite-mourning clothes, alike in
punctuality. Alike in looks, too, if the mumbled
misapprehensions of the mourners were reliable.

"God almighty," Helen said on the evening of the
funeral. "If one person mistook me for Bernie, ten people
did. I must be the spit of her."

Gordon glanced up from his textbook and eyed her
solemnly.

"You want me to tell you there's no resemblance?"

She smiled, caught out.

"OK," he said equably. "There's no resemblance. Bernie
has a withered up oul' crone's puss on her, and you have a
nice, open platthery face."

For a moment now the two faces were close together as
they struggled to get the damp-swollen door open. Helen
pulled the knocker towards her as the key engaged. She
noted the recent tarnish on its surface with the search for
reasons to weep characteristic of the mourner whose initial
agony has softened to a bruised tenderness.

Bernie slid around the door first. The hall was narrow
and the stairs came down so far into its restricted space

that the door never fully opened. For years it had been the old man's habit to open it and stand in the space behind it, silently, waiting for the caller to identify himself. At those times Helen had always felt a huge desire to leap into the space created, telling jokes or tap-dancing.

Now she slid into the musty silence of the place, smiling foolishly. Bernie flipped the light-switch. It was an old fixture, its toggle shaped like an uvula.

"Death-trap this place is. It was always too dark."

Even with the light on, it was coffee-coloured and shadowed. At Helen's back was a plastic relief of Millais' '*Angelus*', a bloom of dust weighing down the two little praying figures.

"We'd better take all the stuff and sort it in one room," Bernie said, removing her dove-grey gloves.

Her suit was slate, shoes and tights charcoal. Helen wondered for an undisciplined second whether her underclothes were also colour coordinated.

"I'll bring the things down from their room," Bernie went on. "Better not have the two of us up there together. It would be just too upsetting."

She climbed the stairs, heavy-footed for such a little woman. Helen watched her, face blank.

"Just *too* upsetting," she mimicked softly to herself, as she turned to go into the kitchen.

She was a silent woman. Silent not by nature, but because the viciousness of her imagined retorts in almost all situations left her shaken and shamed. People thought her shy. They talked to her with that extra gentle slowness they reserve for the shy and for the handicapped whose ailments are not ugly.

Drawers slid and squeaked as she began the inventory. A round wooden biscuit box with a jaunting car in a peeling transfer on the front gave off the barren whisper of stale crumbs. Probably unfilled since the old woman had died a year before.

A good house for grandchildren, it had been. Biscuits pressed on willing toddlers past unheeded parental objections. Mi-wadi ladled with too generous a hand so that it was concentrated and sweet and started little fountains of saliva in the mouth.

In another cubby-hole an old-fashioned lemonade syphon sat beside a new all-purpose version of the same thing. *Sparklets* said the box. Helen ran her finger around the top. The seal was unbroken.

"They had so many things given to them, they didn't know what to be doing with half of them."

Bernie landed a pile of polythene bags with pastel contents down beside the syphon box.

"Most of these she never put on her back."

Each of the polythene bags had a receipt pinned to it. Concessions these to the old woman's choosiness – tickets for a trip to the city, too.

"I have to go and change that blouse Helen gave me," she would say a few weeks after Christmas with a fretful air of duty that fooled no one.

She would make her way to the shop and there happily damn the souls of the sales assistants by looking at every single cardigan they had before picking one only marginally different to the Christmas present. Four years before, she had found herself unable to face even the short journey to the city centre. The pinned receipts had then become small fiscal affirmations of her worth. From that point onward the son and daughters became careless as to style, since she never wore any of the purchases – but careful as to price. The receipt had to show a flatteringly solid outlay.

Bernie pulled out one of the jumpers and smelled it.

"Never worn," she said. "Never worn."

The repetition had a slight vibrato to it.

"I suppose we should just shove all of them in a bag for the Cerebral Palsy shop," Helen suggested.

"The Cerebral Palsy shop?" The vibrato was gone. "Why on earth?"

"Well, do *you* want them?"

An indrawn breath pulled Bernie's mouth into wrinkled folds like a tweaked cord in a drawstring purse.

"Of course not. But they could be changed."

"What?"

"Changed. Exchanged. Someone could bring them back to Arnotts and explain they were never worn."

I don't believe this, Helen thought. I don't believe it. She wants to cash in her old Christmas presents.

"Well, if you can find someone willing to go in and try to exchange things six years old – "

" – but unused – "

" – good luck to you. But it won't be me, I'll tell you that much."

There was a moment's silence.

"It might be better anyway that some good cause got some benefit out of Mammy's things," Bernie conceded, the vibrato back.

Trust you, Helen thought, to make emotional capital out of it. Bernie slid the polythene bags into a plastic sack, pausing every now and then to pat one, which, Helen suspected, had been bought by Bernie herself. Or by one of her children.

"Once all of this is over – "

Bernie's gesture took in the cluttered table, and, by implication, the entire house.

"I will have to get away. The strain's been so intense for so long. I'm at the end of my tether. I have to get away. I just must. It's a question of survival. Survival as a person."

Thank God, Helen thought tangentially, thank God for an impatient husband and an irreverent son who would never let me get away with that kind of rot.

Bernie must never be interrupted. Or jeered at. She watched her sister as she turned over the pages of old Reader's Digests, sniffing the paper as she went. With the total clarity of extreme weariness she accepted that she had never liked Bernie. And now had no reasons left for pretending.

"I am happy though that I felt up to spending so much time with Daddy towards the end," Bernie said. "A good many times when I was alone with him he opened his eyes and looked at me. I think he was glad that I was there. Of course there was nothing I could *do* . . . but just for company."

Helen, stiff-fingered, turned the boxed syphon around and around. Lies, she thought frantically. Lies. The old man *never* opened his eyes towards the end. If he had, he'd never have looked glad to see you. You were two of a kind and he loathed you.

"I'll take that syphon home with me," Bernie said. "I might be able to find some use for it."

Helen's fingers were left squared around a ghost shape as the syphon was lifted.

"I think it must have been a comfort to him."

Only the vibrato indicated the change of topic.

"When he was dying, I stroked his face. Very gently. I stroked his face."

"You stroked his face. You couldn't keep your hands off him. You kept mauling and pawing him, you necrophile. My God, he'd have put you into Kingdom Come if he'd only had the strength."

Helen's voice burbled out in a coarse stream, unstoppable.

"You weren't so great at being around when he was alive and sick and bloody, bloody difficult, but God, when he was dying and silent and comatose and not likely to take a strip off you – oh, yes, *then* you were around. You love death, you vulture you. You love it. Oh God, you love it."

She was crying now, open-mouthed like a slapped child, voice bellowing on every in-breath. Bernie sat silent. Helen dumped her head down among the Reader's Digests and the pastel jumpers and let the raucous tide of her misery vomit out in gradually diminishing eructations.

Eventually there was quiet. Helen geared herself for apologies and self-denigrations. She raised her swollen face. Bernie had gone.

She could hear a car pulling away from the front door. She stumbled to her feet. Dazedly, she looked at the table. The Sparklets syphon was gone. Laughter, turbulent as the tears had been, threatened to topple her. She went to the back door, and clicking the heavy latch, stepped out into the back yard.

It was a tiny overshadowed old garden, cropped-out and bitter. Two apple trees were surrounded by windfalls, wasp and worm-pitted. They were small. She hefted one in her hand. Not a patch on the apples those trees had carried ten, twelve years ago. But perhaps memory was just playing a sentimental tune. She was unsure.

She leaned against a branch, crooning softly for comfort. She felt naked and raw as if a skin had been peeled away.

We come double-wrapped for better protection in our parents, she thought. When they die, we are exposed. To death. That bit more vulnerable. Guilt followed the thought. She lay against the roughness of the tree bark, swallowing to clear the ache in her throat.

The pear tree looked defeated. It had never held fruit except the year her father had tied five small green pears to it to fool her mother who owned it.

The pretence had been kept up for weeks while the

pears turned yellow and soft.

Not out of kindness on the old man's part; he had none in his patrician make-up. A perceptive and ruthless humour had been at the back of it, Helen decided, and a weakening sympathy for the dead old woman brought her close to tears again.

She made her way across the uneven cement to the big outdoor larder, a wooden construction with thickly opaque wire netting to guard against cats and insects.

The door was stuck. She thumped the catch, and it sprang open. Dust-mites danced out into the sunlight. At the front of the bottom shelf potatoes sprouted tall leafy plants. Some had lain against the door, and with its withdrawal, their foliage waved freely at her. Behind the potatoes was something exuding a throat-catching putrid sweetness – something round and furred with corruption.

"That's someone else's problem," she said aloud, and closed the door on them.

The Intervention

She was insecure rather than uncomfortable. The head rest was narrow so that if she moved her head to one side or the other she had no support. Five minutes before she had begun to want to change her position and the thought had since then dilated into importance in her mind. If she moved at all she would have her hip pressed into a groove by the gear stick. She would probably knock down some of the small rattling things he kept in the little tray beside the gear lever. His pipe was there, and a three-legged instrument which had something to do with the pipe, and a dirty white furry pipe-cleaner which she had twisted into the shape of a pair of spectacles. There was a lipstick which she had never missed, and a little purse, with 'My Rosary' on it in gold letters which were beginning to peel off.

"Where did you get the rosary?"

It took him a minute to locate it.

"Oh. An old aunt of mine. She thinks you should pray in traffic jams."

He reached down and came up with the lipstick, rolling it in his palm the way her dentist used to roll the mercury particles when, as a child, she had been frightened of the drill.

"I never know what I'm going to find after you get out. I search the car from top to bottom for hairpins, lipsticks, tins of saccharin, everything."

"You're lucky I don't leave anything more incriminating."

She was hurt that he should excise the traces of her being there. It was like the way he would pull his shirt away from his chest at the end of an evening spent in her company. He would look down at it, pull his head into his neck so that he had a momentary double-chin, in order to see if there were make-up stains on the fabric. She pushed the lipstick into her pocket. It was without a lid, and bits of grit from the interior of the pocket would stick to it. She shifted slightly, careful not to touch the little tray.

"What're you thinking?"

"Wondering if I made the pipe-cleaner grubby, playing with it."

She nodded towards the tray. The fringe of the rug he had wrapped around them pulled loose and a long woollen finger poked at her mouth. She nodded her head at it ineffectually. After a few seconds his hand came over and tucked it underneath. A heavy moth knocked against the windscreen. Gerard moved to turn off the interior light. She stopped him.

"I want to see you."

"You don't mind if my battery runs down?"

"To hell with your battery."

He laughed and then suddenly became serious.

"I missed you terribly."

She nodded, aware of a growing stiffness in her neck.

"Do you know how much I missed you?"

The question embarrassed her. She wondered how best to respond. Men were never demonstrative like this. *She* was the one who ought to be telling him how much she had missed him. With anybody else, she would have dredged up incidents from the last few days to decorate the picture of her loneliness. But here with him all she wanted to do was to sit quietly as if by disturbing the silence she could cause him to find her out. She had consciously faked an image of herself in every other relationship, and she was now obsessed by fear that Gerard would somehow see through her honesty.

"Your arm can't be comfortable." She nudged it with the back of her head.

"It's beautiful," he said impatiently.

"I know it's beautiful, but it's not comfortable."

He didn't smile. After a moment his expression changed and she rushed into speech to stave off whatever mood might take over.

"I couldn't get a picture of you while you were away."

He didn't understand. She explained about late nights when she had tried to envisage his face, and the features, created separately by her imagination, failed to coalesce into the whole image. She told it badly and he asked her why she hadn't looked at his photograph.

The awkwardness of her position made concentration difficult. She suddenly spurted out her need to move and surged over on to one side. The rug came with her and the backs of her legs were suddenly cold. She wanted to rearrange it, but lay still for a while.

She was a big girl, tall and heavy and the way the well-sprung car weaved lightly on its wheels when she moved worried her. She had a theory that the reason fat people were unpopular was because they disturbed other people's ration of air and so she moved more quietly than a slender girl, with a curious swimming glide. In the enclosed space she seemed to herself to be huge. It made her more grateful to him for liking her.

"It's not the most comfortable, is it?" Gerard looked around the dark interior of the car as if he could stretch it.

"Well, at least it has let-down seats."

He laughed and snuggled his head into her shoulder.

"My mother would be horrified."

"Would she think you'd spend the night in a car with a man?"

"Oh, much worse. My mother is very right-wing. She has a very dirty mind."

They laughed and he moved his head in the warmth of her neck again, like a baby pushing deeper into its mother's flesh. The smell of his clean hair was spicy in her nostrils and she tried to identify his shampoo by the perfume. Disturbed by her silence, he asked her what her thoughts were, and she felt compelled to hide their inanity.

"Just wondering what your mother will think of me."

"Oh, she'll like you. She'll like you very much. Oh, she will. And you'll like her, too."

He reached up unexpectedly and turned out the light. For a few seconds his face-shape hovered indistinctly above her in the total darkness, and then it developed an outline and features in the half-light provided by some unseen moon. His eyes had no points of light in them. They would be difficult to sketch. If you put highlights into pictures of the eyes, or even reflected windows, they always looked alive. She pulled her hand out from beneath the rug and touched his face, finding the narrow strip of softer skin between his short side-burns and his ear. He looked at her almost wistfully.

"There's something very elusive about you," he said. "I don't think I know you at all sometimes."

Her hand pressed against his cheek, she hesitated, undecided whether to deny it as she wanted to or leave the impression which, though false, was better than that he should think of her as being as obvious as a billboard. The pause deteriorated into silence and he lay down beside her again. After a while she asked him what he had done in the evenings when he had been away. He said "nothing", and she knew that he had wanted her mind to have been turning on something nearer to their relationship. His hand moved gently on her thigh and the satin lining of her skirt followed the movement, stroking her skin with an oddly comfortable whisper.

She moved her mouth and nose gently in his hair, and he settled a little closer as if reassured by the touch. Before she needed to breathe in, she raised her head and looked vaguely around the inside of the big car.

There was a face, black in silhouette, a foot away from hers, pressed into idiocy against the window-glass.

Her breath sucked in through her throat and was expelled in a bawling roar which sickened her. Her rearing upwards brought her nearer to the face and the car was suddenly alive with the wobbling light of a torch. Gerard instantly reacted. His hand came up from under the rug and banged on the window. He shouted.

The face, blacker now and more menacing behind the torch-circle, roared something in an inarticulate furious growl. It sounded like "Get out of it." It seemed to her that the three of them were going to be suspended in this minute of terror for ever and then the rug was flung back over her, the torch went out and a cold wind swept in through the car door as Gerard leaped out. She made a grab at the end of his jacket but her fingers were tangled in the rug and the fringe-fingers waved at him with inconsequent cheerfulness as he disappeared. His own footsteps ran after him into the silence.

"Don't hit him," she said fiercely, in a whisper, pulling the rug around her. "Don't hit him please don't hit him don't hit him."

She kept her eyes away from the rear-view mirror but listened so hard that the blood hummed in her ears. The backs of her legs were shaking. She found herself stroking the polo-neck of her sweater as if to assure herself that she was not naked but felt even more sordid because she was dressed. The footsteps walked back out of the silence.

Gerard pulled open the door of the car and slid into the seat beside her, looking back.

"Did you hit him?"

He was breathing heavily, whether from running or from fury she couldn't tell.

"Did you *hit* him?"

"Lord, no," he said. He looked at her with surprise. "Lord, no, I didn't hit him. I'd never have hit the poor bugger."

He gathered the rug around her and she was surprised by his ability to do it gently. She had expected the violence to overflow. He held the doubled edge of it on either side of her face and pulled her close to him. She felt as comforted and safe as when her mother had trussed her in a big towel as a child after a bath.

"Were you frightened?"

She nodded too many times.

"Ah, my little love," he said, and the inaccuracy made the big girl cry, where fright had left her dry-eyed.

Her hands were pinned to her side by the tightness of the rug-wrapping. When she sobbed she moved all of a piece in his arms. Later, when the sobs were like dying hiccups she said that she thought he would kill the man, that anyway she thought the man was a garda. He asked her what a garda would be doing at a deserted inlet of the sea at that hour. She lay, numbed by her own stupidity, waiting for the next sob.

"I'd never have hit the poor bugger," he said again. She asked him why he had chased him.

"Oh, I might have chuckled him."

"Chuckled him?"

"That's a great spake in our part of the country," he told

her, smiling. "When you chuckle a fella, you get him like this – "

Gerard grabbed the edges of the rug as if they were the lapels of a man's jacket, and dragged her up against his chest. Her head fell back and the tears came again at the sudden roughness. He looked at her as if she puzzled him and then, holding her in one arm, he fingered the edge of the seat until he found the lever, and pulled it. The seatback sprang into place so smartly that it walloped him in the back. He sat upright and pulled her over so that her head was in his lap, eyes looking up at him. She loved to do this for his face looked heavier from that angle. She always thought he looked too thin.

He stroked her forehead until the furrows of caring smoothed out, and then he slid his hand through the steering wheel and picked up the packet of cigarettes and lighter from the dashboard. He lit a cigarette and blew smoke towards the ceiling, and then looked down at her.

"Did you think I was going to kill him?"

"Yes."

"Ah, no. Sure that poor oul' fella probably can't help it. My God, if he has to wait until three in the morning to get his thrills . . . can you imagine walking around here in the cold, hoping for a courting couple to show up?"

She did not want them to be lumped together with courting couples but could find no words to express her jealous guarding of their uniqueness. Her head bobbed in his lap as he laughed noiselessly.

"I suppose he thought with the two of us under the rug that we were both stark naked. He must have got the fright of his life when he found that the man in the case was well able to make a run after him!"

He drew on the cigarette.

"The fright of his life, he must have got."

She liked this habit he had of repeating phrases like the

chorus of a song. It gave her a feeling of ease in his company to know he would delay his thoughts by this little trick and that she could keep up with him.

"I'm sorry for roaring like that," she said, trying to locate the deep discomfort in herself.

"I didn't notice," he said absently. He opened the small side window and flicked the cigarette butt off his thumb with his forefinger. She sat up.

"Let's go," he said, and she knew that he was not sure whether he meant to take her home or to drive her somewhere else.

When he turned the key slowly, the lights came on before the engine caught and the long reeds at the water's edge sprang into reality as silver rods. He looked at her, his face bright with reflected light. The engine drilled the silence. With the gear in neutral, he shook another cigarette from the packet and crouched, squinting, for her to hold the lighter-flame to it.

Then the car moved slowly off the rough ground, and the headlamps mowed a narrow path between the long grasses.

O'GRADY SAYS

YOU WAKE AS A DOLL YOU HAD YEARS AGO USED TO WAKE: abruptly wide-eyed. The doll was a too-pretty baby. A ridge of black eyelashes above each eye was glued together and chopped off uniformly. Sitting her up made the eyes clunk to openness.

You do not sit up. You lie, flat on your back, hands already touching your breasts. A touch, not a fondle. Examination in search of data. Result: flaccid. As if slightly deflated.

Your hands move on to the hardness of hip bones, pleased that the padded presence of stomach has given way to a downward swing of skin, stretched between each hip promontory like a hammock.

Your very quietness as you move towards the bathroom on the landing distinguishes you from the others in this house. So does the tap water you turn on as soon as the door is locked with you on the inside. Your steps thereafter are sequential, consequential. Miss one, and you are vexed by the impossibility of a revision.

First, you weigh yourself with dressing-gown on. 122, says the scale. You brought it back from Orlando. The others brought rollerblades and soft souvenir Disney characters. Now, the red digital figures drop away, leaving

the small window black. You shed the dressing-gown and
try again. 121. Then you sit on the toilet, push-voiding like
an obedient toddler at training time. You do not flush the
toilet before going back on the scale. 121. You stand on it,
possessed by a hectic fury that demands splintering of
mirrors, hammering at hard hollow surfaces all around you.
But you smile bleakly at your reflection as you step off.

The tap-water is still flowing. You clean your teeth with
a vigour and a venom unrequired by the task. You rinse,
seething water through the minuscule gaps in your teeth
and spit out every trace of toothpaste. This last is a recent
addition to your morning liturgy, since you heard someone
talking on the radio about a terrorist who had undertaken a
highly-publicised hunger strike in prison yet – according to
a sniggering warder – had assuaged his hunger at dawn
and dusk with swallowed toothpaste. When you heard that
you rushed to read the label on the tube. Cellulose gum
probably had calories, you decided, and glycerine was
some kind of fat, you had seen it listed in moisturising
creams. The fact that saccharin was named on it was
probably a blind.

You sit on the toilet again to produce a trickle, silent
against the still-running tap. Then you take off the T-shirt
and underpants you sleep in and step on the scale again.
120. To make absolutely sure you step on and off three
times with a hesitation each time, to allow it to turn itself
off between weighings. It is like a stylised march. The last
time you come down heavily on the bathroom floor tiles
with your heels. 120. It will flutter into red digital life in
your mind's eye all day, just as a melody will recur over a
number of hours. You had hoped for 119.

The double-digit change is always magical, a triumph to
be hugged to the chest. Without it, today, there must be
others. You pull back on the T-shirt and pants (you never
look at yourself naked), and face the mirror square on and

raise your arms to shoulder level. The plumpness of a few months ago has gone, as has the hanging emptiness of more recent weeks. Now there is a nugget of hardened muscle and when you pinch the skin over that nugget your fingers almost meet. Drop the arms and they fall tightly parallel to the body like square brackets. You can remember when the roundness of the upper arm met the pad of fat over your upper rib cage (like a continuation, you would think bitterly, of your breasts under your arms). Your arms were forced out from your body. Weight-lifter's walk, you said you had.

You look at yourself sideways in the mirror. At this point there is nothing at your sides but shadowed depressions between ribs. You fill your lungs with air to make the depressions more apparent. Even if you lay down flat on your back your breasts would sit, flattened like small poached eggs, rather than surging burgeoning globes.

You consider sitting on the toilet again and stripping off the T-shirt but you decide you do not deserve this concession. You turn the tap off and go back to your bedroom. This used to be the time to pull on sweat-pants, a top and running shoes, and head out into the damp dawn to run yourself into heart-pounding, head-pounding, blood-pounding control of the day. But they have banned that and it is impossible to get out without being caught.

So instead you put your dressing-gown on the floor plus your coat, to deaden sound, and you start with flutter-kicks. You keep your heels a few inches off the ground with your legs stiff while you raise one foot to eye level, then the other, one hundred times in a row. Dragging hot-wire pain comes after sixty of them. You push against it, making the 'kicks' slower and slower to force the muscles to do more and more work.

After flutter-kicks comes cycling in the air. One hundred

repetitions. Then you stand to do the tricep hammers to tone up the softness below your upper arms. They took away your dumbbells a while back, but the outside advisers have always stressed the importance of your privacy ("within reason, of *course* . . . "). And so they have never noticed that two of the thick white towelling socks in your drawer are knotted – separately – at the ankle to hold in the four hundred twopences that add up to 3 kilograms. The weighted socks, held firmly to prevent the possibility of a chinking of coin, are raised above your head, dropped behind your back, over and over again. You count the repetitions. When you feel you haven't given full value by pushing the arm down along your spine as far as you can, or allowed natural momentum to push the weight, as opposed to direct muscle power, you punish yourself by adding another set of twenty repetitions to the total. Sometimes, the additions keep you at it until the family are all up and moving around. On a couple of occasions, you have been tempted to claim sickness in order to complete the growing exigence of the mathematics, but claiming sickness is likely to draw them on you. So you simply get up early enough to commit yourself to all the possible variations.

Today, because it is the start of the half-term break, there is a luxury to the process. You know that you are likely to have the house to yourself later and will be able to repeat it many times. By nightfall your every movement will be a relish of tender muscle groups.

There are others in this house but they have become to you like trick three-dimensional pictures. Look directly at the picture and it is full of busy detail, but train your eye to look through the picture and you see the hidden horse, the trees and mountains. You can see the others in the house, if you concentrate, but there is a busy detail in the foreground of the picture that makes them almost invisible.

It is as if they know themselves to be invisible, too. The house has become quieter. There used to be banged doors and shouted huffiness, much competition of music as a ghetto-blaster in one room fought to silence a cassette-player in another.

But a reverence descended about eighteen months ago. (Now, you are rolling your Vaseline'd knuckles down along your thighs as if you could flatten the curve by force. This, according to the magazine from which you got the idea, "helps to break up deposits of fat".)

The reverence was preceded by battle royal. That was what your father called it. Battle royal. Do we have to have battle royal ever single day in this household? Over every single shagging meal? Jesus, are we to have another battle royal over tea-time, same as we did over breakfast?

Battle royal didn't directly involve you. It was fought about you, around you and over you in terms you barely understood. You listened as you would to a radio commercial for a new food product; with mild distant interest. They talked of you as looking like something out of Belsen. You didn't know where Belsen was. Nor did you ask. The process you had embarked upon tended to do away with spare time and curiosity. Your mother and father came close to blaming each other. If you hadn't always been going on about – well, if *you* hadn't used such awful discouraging jokes. And as for the two of *you*, with your adolescent smart cracks at people's sore points . . .

At the beginning of battle royal, your parents still had a presumed power. When you've finished your schooling, they would say, when you have a flat of your own, then you can behave whatever way you want. But as long as you're under *my* roof. Or they would stage family meals, forbidding the grazing that everybody had got used to because of differing times of arrival in the house. The staged family meals were the worst. The younger ones, at that point, were not clued in to what was going on, and so you had to try to follow their random conversation while doing the sums in your head. You would be halfway through a totting-up of fat grams when you would be asked a question, and the younger ones would mimic Day-Lewis's Christy, head tilted, mouth agape, to mock your stumped expression. It was only when they forced you to eat that way that you got rid of it afterwards. It was the only way to retrieve the situation if they took control from you. Other than that period, you relied on self-discipline and exercise.

That period proved to your parents how powerless they really were. They handed you over. The handing over should have made you hate them but it is difficult to hate when you are busy about many things. It is difficult to hate people who are receding from peoplehood as you watch the details in the foreground of the picture.

The professionals were quite different. They had been there before. They were pleasant. They knew your systems before you told them. They did specious deals with you, calm in the knowledge that they had all of the power. They supplanted your liturgy with another. They talked at you in ways that forced you to respond so that you lost the string of your thoughts and your sums.

The others in your home were ambivalent about the hospitalisation. You heard your father mutter at one stage that if parents regimented kids the way hospitals regiment kids, they'd be had up, maybe convicted of some kind of abuse. But they were grateful, too, your mother and father. Grateful for the humiliation of being invited to cheerlead for every added pound, and for the fact that nobody blamed them. Your mother bought books and followed different theories. One said it was a form of slow suicide, a withdrawal from social contact, another that it was a rejection of voluptuous bountiful womanhood. The book-learning and the theories separated one parent from the other. Your mother wanted to understand. Your father just wanted the whole thing over. No. He wanted the whole thing never to have happened in the first place.

This morning, there are sounds in the house and you are getting dressed. It is springtime but you wear more clothes than the season calls for. You are chilly, for one thing. Constantly chilly, blue-fingernailed and slowed by the cold. And extra layers conceal how thin you have become. You know you are thinner, but you would never describe yourself as "thin". When you were 150, you thought you would when you were 140. Now, you think you might be thin at 110.

But you don't know. That's not the objective, anyway. The objective is the daily score. The progress. The sense of space within waistbands. The spare sketchiness of your facial structure as it emerges from the months of hospital force-feeding and post-hospital obedience.

You go downstairs. Three of them are in the kitchen, eager to get through breakfast, unable to be boastfully unashamed as once they were of their hunger or joyous in food demolition. You load a bowl with All-Bran and make yourself herb tea.

Herb tea requires no milk, and there is still a satisfaction in you for outwitting them on this choice. You presented it as being for your recurrent sniffles. You produced in support, a newspaper feature by an allergist who claimed that Irish people cause themselves many problems in the nasal passages by eating too many dairy foods. There were quick sneaky glances between your brothers, but they were not going to scoff and draw down disaster, so it was let pass.

You move to the table and sit down where they can see you pour milk from the ordinary milk jug into the All-Bran. This, too, is a system. You put the pointed nose of the jug close to the bowl and they see white pour from one to the other, but they don't see how little. They do not realise that the bottom half-inch of All-Bran soaks up the milk and you never eat the fat-soaked bottom layer. You eat the rest of it, dry match-stick in texture, drinking herb tea the while.

You think about what you will do when they are gone. You might run up and down the stairs a set number of times. Or dance. You might have a long bath and rub away any rough skin on your arms with a loofah, and on your feet with a pumice stone. You might lose several ounces that way. You know that this is not rational, but it is pleasing and sometimes efficacious. You are also considering going into town and giving blood. This is a new idea and you are somewhat daunted by the possibility that the Blood Bank might inform on you.

They watch you out of the sides of their eyes, and you know they watch you. In reshaping your body, you are reshaping all of their lives. There is no intent to it. No awareness of it. No pleasure in it for you. They are innocent bystanders injured in your war.

Your father used to have a reactive humour of summaries and puns. It spurted into one final foray in a session in the hospital when a therapist asked him to summarise his perception of what had happened in the family as a result of this illness. "Fear of Frying," came the definition. There was a wash of self-reproachful desperation when the other participants in the group wrote him off as facetious and uncaring. He was neither. Afterwards he sought refuge in a slow-moving formality reminiscent of the approach taken by a corporation that wants to get rid of someone but is at pains not to provide the staffer with the evidence on which to sue for Constructive Dismissal. The formality came with him wherever he went. At home, "yer ma" was modulated into "your mother." Shortened names grew extra syllables and seriousness.

One of the younger ones had come to the age where the jokes refer to body processes and distortions. What, he asked one day, what do you call a man with no arms and no legs, floating in a swimming pool? (You did not seek to come up with the answer. The others did. You, on the other hand, worked out how many pounds would be accounted for in weighing a man without arms and legs.) When nobody responded, he roared with laughter. Bob, he yelled. Bob! D'you see? Your father looked at him with such baffled rage that the kid was frightened into retreat. Permanent retreat.

The definition of it as an illness made it less intimidating to the younger ones, although they still became quieter, afraid that their noisy ordinariness would somehow rupture the membrane of your medically-defined misery.

Except, to you, it is neither illness nor misery. It is a solution, an explanation, a code to live by. Its triumphs, some of them, are simple. Tomorrow morning at 5.30, if the red digital figures show a drop, that is a triumph. Other triumphs are more complex, more tied in with the distancing of the others. There is, for example, the double duplicity of this morning's breakfast. You are adding cornflakes to the half-eaten bowl of All-Bran. You know it puts them off the track, and the older ones are getting back on the track, troubled by the down beginning to appear on your obviously thinner face. But an extra serving of cornflakes, voluntarily ingested, while they watch?

Later, you will eat three bowls of diabetic jelly. They have yet to catch on to that one. They never reckoned that you would take refuge in the formal terms of your surrender. "I will never again buy or eat Ex-Lax chocolate laxative." Those were your preferred terms, but they were too quick for that. They changed the wording and made you say it out loud. "I will never again buy or swallow any laxative." They would never have thought of sorbitol in diabetic jelly, or known that if you eat enough of it, it has the same effect as a dose of laxative. Your expertise, your ostensible honesty defeated and continue to defeat them. As does your politeness.

You were always the model of goodchild behaviour. They watched you in delight, one Christmas, when all of the pre-teens but you were tumbling and howling. You had been given a gadget shaped like opera-glasses, into which was inserted a disc of bright fingernail-sized colour slides. When you looked through the eye-pieces, the slides sprang into a vivid circle of bright stills from a recently-released movie starring the Muppets. You found the mechanism difficult but once you had come to terms with it, you retreated into rapt, slow-breathing absence. Outside the contained vividness in your hands was nothing comparably real. Now, outside the overwhelming logic and satisfaction of this sectioned process towards suicide, there is nothing comparably real. It dwarfs the claims and presence of others. Your mother goes to work each day puzzled by a pleasurable sensation of helplessness. She has always managed the lives around her, but yours defeats her, and the defeat is a freedom. The impotent are not expected to make the earth move for others, and are not blamed when it doesn't.

Parents always seek to imprison children in the past. You have succeeded in imprisoning this whole household in the present. There is no future. Just today with its observances. If you live, the younger ones will get away physically and the older ones will get away some other way. If you die, the older ones will retreat from each other in desperation, and the younger ones will have had their lone identity stolen from them. They will always be the brothers of the girl who . . . The morbidly affiliative Irish mindset will see to that. They will be dogged by days whose intensely cherished happiness is predicated on the certainty of future misery.

They are gone, now, your family. Gone to the day jobs. But the evening will come quickly, sped toward you by the tasks you must complete, and they will return. That is the uniqueness of this sustained stick-up. Without wanting to lead, you dictate their moves. Without caring about it, you have them as players in your version of the kids' game, "O'Grady Says".

O'Grady says do this.

THE CHOSEN DESERT

HE VISUALISED WHERE HE WAS GOING FROM AS IF FROM ABOVE AS he always did when driving, It would look, this place, like a plus sign set down inside a big oblong. The plus sign the shopping mall itself. The oblong the car park. It pleased him to envision a flashing red arrow and the words *You are here.*

The arrow would point to a parking spot. Not the same parking spot as last week. This week the '76 Chevy Monte Carlo was positioned near the south entrance to the mall. The one with the alligators in neon outline. To distinguish it from the north entrance, where there were blue dolphins, the east entrance, where there were brown lizards, and the west entrance, where there were flamingoes posed on one leg. The alligators were the same colour as the green luminous figures on his watch when he looked at it in the dark. They were reproduced in reflective accuracy by the great puddles in the wet black tarmac.

The pick-up trucks were beginning to arrive. Early beer-drinkers, windows down, cabs vibrating to radio music turned up as loud as it would go. Bumper-stickers making statements.

"I didn't elect *her,*" one of them stated.

Long denimed legs. Heavy engraved metal belt buckles. Cowboy boots. Cowboy hats too on some of them. A group of teenage girls arrived together, all slender, all with straight blonde long hair. All wearing white cowboy hats. They stood with the tops of their fingers jammed into front or back jeans pockets, elbows out at an angle. Their angles interlinked like a fence made up of diamond-shaped wire.

His windows were rolled down on either side. The AC had never worked and so the creation of a draught was the best that could be achieved on days such as these. These were the dog days of summer. The days when, even before the sun came up, going out in the open meant being slapped in the face by an atmosphere as hot and heavily damp as a face-cloth. By noon the temperature gauges outside the bank would say 97°. By early afternoon, a lowering headache was a portent of the storm to come.

The storms were an ecstasy to him. At home, storms had been occasional. During holidays in Laytown, groups sitting strumming guitars on the front veranda of the wooden holiday homes had sometimes watched the lightning dancing onto the sea and counted the beats before the thunder rolled, comparing the noise of each clap and reassuring the small children who were scared by something they could see was not only outside parental control, but creative of fear in parents they needed to know no fear. He could remember that happening twice or three times.

But here the storms came with clockwork regularity, undiminished in their elemental threat by daily manifestation. Clouds gathered after three, and by half four (he mentally corrected the phrase to 'four-thirty') the distant warning grumbles were peals so loud that they carried a shockwave before them. The sky would darken so definitively it was difficult to imagine it had ever been blue and bright. Waves of electric air would lift the hairs on his forearms. The air, all day, would have been stony-still and heavy as a blood-filled sponge, now it would whisper and vacillate, growing into a scurried breeze, then a wild wind at a run from the coming storm, which flattened and flurried the broad-leaved grass before it, scoring texture across the smoothness of the lakes.

Sometimes sheet lightning brightened everything with a shocking cold sky-filled surge. More often forked lightning; split, sharpened fissures through the clouds unlikely in their artistry and duration. The thunder now and then broke directly overhead, unaugured by a lightning strike and the impact would almost drive him to his knees.

Mostly, though, he could follow the arced life of it to its climax, where flash and thunderclap came together in a great impersonal shock of power, vibrating the floor of his trailer home and trembling his blood.

It would come with rain the like of which he had never seen. Rain that was an attack so hard, so sure, that a running retreat was the only response. The shoppers would come out of the malls and stand, bright bags in hand, surprised by the scale and fury of it. Car keys would be rooted out of pocket books and trousers, and the door key separated from the others. Then they would wait for a flash and a roar and use that as the starting point to a wild run for their car.

Even if that car were only twenty yards away, they tumbled into it breathless from the run, shirts and dresses soaked through, jeans turned dark and heavy, runnels trailing around ankles and down, down, to pool noisily inside shoes.

He would become timelessly engrossed by it, as he sat on a wooden bench seat at a mall sheltered by an overhanging roof made of heavy plastic. The noise forced everybody in the dry area to make friendly shouts at each other.

He would watch the angled rods against the dark slate grey of the sky, try to follow them to the ground, see their force spark splashes off the tarmac. Nearer to where he sat, the rain would fall squabblingly into the tough rubbery leaves of the shrub-bank, the red tropical flowers beaten, but never into subjection. As the onslaught diminished, the flowers would shiver and revive in the cooler air. Cooler by ten or fifteen degrees, he found. Every time the rain lost power and the noise went somewhere else, he could hear in his head the quiet bit at the end of the Pastorale. His mother – a music teacher – had introduced them all to music as more than melody and camaraderie by playing them pieces that told a story. The uncanny accuracy of that piece gave him a feeling that only he and Beethoven had experienced a particular kind of storm – and a gladness that his isolation prevented him ever giving voice to vapidities he could not stop his mind enjoying.

Sometimes there was sunshine and a spectacular sunset after the storm. Tonight, darkness followed quickly. The lights under the canopies picked up the fluorescent pinks and greens of the shorts, sparked off spangles and sequins and grape-sized jewels of purple, ruby and emerald. The beading, the flying fringing and the heavy turquoise and silver bangles on the men were like school badges or altar albs: sacramental signs of submersion in a greater identity.

Now would be a good time to go in, he figured. There would still be lots of little tables unoccupied but enough people there busy greeting each other and trying out steps at the corner of the dancing area. He would not be noticed.

Nobody watched him as he got out of the car. It was a big, grey, boat-shaped car, its body-paint oxidised to non-reflective matt, its windows darkened from the inside by some previous owner so that it always looked unoccupied.

Even when he was driving it sedately along, as he had learned years before in a stolen Toyota.

Don't be noticeable. Don't attract attention. Drive too fast, they spot you. Drive too slow, they spot you. Be bloody invisible, all right? You didn't get into this to show off. That's for wee kids in their daddy's car at the weekend. When you have to, you'll drive fast. When you don't have to, you'll drive like a little old lady. Clear?

He still drove like a little old lady. The vast over-sprung Chevy met speed bumps with the overstated patronage of a dowager bowing to a social inferior. The big car rarely got above forty miles an hour, and got to that speed by a seamless graduation of pace. A few months before he discovered a nest of baby mice when he cleaned out the back seat area. (Nobody ever sat in the car but himself.) The family had been travelling with him, undisturbed, for some weeks.

The grill/bar was half-full, its darker seating areas surrounded a dance-floor done in draught-board black and white squares. In one corner of the dance-floor was a raised stage decorated by neon outlines of guitars and saxophones and flying notes of music, where the disc jockey stood. Tonight it was Gator Murtry from the local radio station ("more music, less talk"/"the hottest country music").

A boat with no wake, the man attracted no attention as he found a small round table and sat, casually tilting the other chair so that it joined the unoccupied team at the next table and minimised the chances of anyone joining him.

A few couples moved in time to the music at the edge of the dance-floor. Some of them he recognised. He had titles for the regulars. There was the Widow, although she didn't seem to be here, yet, tonight. There was the Banker, a solidly overweight six-footer in soft canvas shoes and shorts, who danced without facial expression as if he was involved only by accident. There was the Mailman, a tall thin young man with the angular free-leggedness of a foal. The Mailman was explaining a step to a newcomer, their long-toed cowboy boots lined up in parallel as she mimicked him.

"What can I git for *you*, right now, Sir?"

The waiter wore a black satin anorak and despite the tonal enthusiasm of his question looked into the middle distance, as always.

"Burger. Plain. Rare. Coke no ice."

"Right away, Sir," he said, laying down a paper napkin in something of a statement of intent.

Beside the Mailman in comic contrast, was the Eyes-man. The Eyes-man was shaped as if he had been intended to be six foot six in height, but at the last moment had had a heavy weight lowered on him, forcing the bulk of him down. He was as bellied and buttocked as an eighteenth-century cartoon, belted bravely in strong leather and topped by a black cowboy hat, under whose rim his eyes popped like pale marbles ready to spring from the sockets, each staring, independent of the other, one to the right, one to the left. The Eyes-man was terrifying in appearance and had an almost crippled awkwardness of gait. He walked in a disconnected set of overlapping wobbles.

On a dance-floor, though, he was as transformed as a penguin is in water. He danced easily and well, accurate in his footwork. At the moment, he was jiving with one of the slender blonde white-hatted teenagers, his gaze bizarre in its truncation, his grin manic. The girl was expressionless and gum-chewing, and he was spinning and running her at the end of his stubby arms with an impersonal confidence and authority marvellous to watch. He drove her under the arch made by their raised, joined hands, then folded her to herself so that her arms crossed on her chest like the plaster statue of the Madonna which used to stand on the mantelpiece at home.

"One burger, rare, and one Coke no ice," the waiter announced. "Anything else I can get for you, Sir?"

He shook his head and the waiter went away. Today, he realised, he had only had to use his voice once. Sometimes, he managed all day without his voice ever being heard or his silence noticed.

Voices are as distinctive as fingerprints, they had trained him to realise. The words you use. The syllables you inflect. The answers you give. Talk's cheap. And dangerous. They can't catch you for what you don't say. Let the others talk – they'll be glad to.

The dance-trainer had arrived and was fitting his electronic microphone around his stetson so that it would be positioned in front of his mouth as he danced. His casual tests of its function interrupted the song.

The silent man loved the naked sentiment of the country songs, with their cold cups of coffee, their throaty betrayals and their bumper-sticker philosophies.

Sometimes you're the Louisville Slugger,
Sometimes you're the ball –

"Testing, testing, tk tk tk-"

Sometimes you're the windshield,
Sometimes you're the bug,
Sometimes it all comes together –
Sometimes you're a fool in love.

"Aw right then," the dance tutor said with unfelt vigour. "Anyone here last Toosday when we were doing the line dance to Black Velvet, whyncha c'mon down here and join us. We're gonna review what we did last week, learn a few little new steps and – hey – then we're gonna put it all together."

There was a rush of dancers to the checkerboard floor. The silent man spotted the grandmother and her granddaughter, the older woman no taller than the twelve-year-old, and dressed in twelve-year-old's clothes, the weathered face a pale statement of incongruity over a white blouse with cut-outs at the shoulder, a bleached blue denim skirt tiered in lace, and white ankle boots with flying fringes. The Banker, the Eyes-man and the Banker's sexy younger wife, packed roundly into tight black shorts and a jewelled black T-shirt: they were all there.

"So how are *you*?"

He turned slowly. The Widow was there, twinkling at him. Slender in jeans and a gingham blouse, her hand on the back of the spare chair at his table. He smiled at her without speaking, then nodded his head questioningly towards the dance-floor.

"No, I don't like that one," she said. "Are we going to see *you* out on the floor tonight?"

He shook his head and an empty pause floated, unowned, between them. Then she palm-patted the back of the chair she had been leaning on and walked away to friends on the other side of the bar.

He ate his hamburger and watched the dancers being corrected when they made missteps. This, he decided, would be the last time he would come here. Or go to any place where they did country in-line dancing. Because there was a community forming and a recognition building. He lifted his empty plate and put it on an unoccupied table behind him. That, too, was a habit of training.

It's like scuffing over your footprints. Nobody might ever notice but you should nevertheless confuse the picture for anyone who might want to re-construct it afterwards.

The lesson finished, and the tutor was introducing a line dance. From all around the silent man, they came. All ages, they were. Some newcomers. Some in thong sandals or sneakers. Some old hands. The lines formed without dictation from a central source. Short people beside other short people, but also dwarfed by the tall dancers. Skirts beside shorts and shorts beside jeans. Little acknowledgement of others, each dancer at pains to respect the other's envelope of space.

The disc jockey identified the record he was about to play and it whammed into the space, louder than the music used for the lesson. Instantly the lines of individuals became a unity of practised movement. Three steps to the right, he knew, was a "right vine", and there was much of that, followed by dips, skips, and four angled turns. The less experienced dancers kept to the outside lines where they stood less chance of getting in someone's way. The rank newcomers were to be spotted at the edges, often facing oncoming lines of dancers, gazing fixedly at the advancing feet, trying to come to terms with the movements.

He watched with a pleasure already tinged with nostalgia, registering for future reference the unflurried, uninvolved look of the Banker who, from the waist up, might have been conducting a meeting about lending, while his soft-shod feet met each beat of the music gracefully. The woman who usually came with the Banker danced with an assertive sexiness of hip and an unashamed pleasure in her own raunchiness. The Mailman, long-legged and spiky; a man without need for group admiration, did an earnest solo to shared music.

The silent man watched and wondered what he would do instead of coming here. It was the speculation that was the reward, he knew. Five years without regimentation or involvement with anybody and he still did take for granted the pleasurable selfishness of it. He could go anywhere at any time and be answerable to nobody. Up to then, his life had always been bucketed down a tube he knew, a tube tunnelled out as bobsleds tunnel a path for themselves in ice.

It wasn't that he had known the road, when he was a child. It was that the road shaped and sang with them as the car went along, as he looked at the farm buildings and listened for the themes in his father's talk. The mention of Mickey McVerry and the death he had died. Over there.

Up in that corner, see?

His mother was inconsistent in her shushing of his father, and so, as they would go into Newtownhamilton, just as he read the names – *Mone, Rice, Irwins* – off the shopfronts, he would wait for his father's voice to make a jagged noise like a throat-clearing. Now and again, there was no more than the jagged noise. The boy in the back of the car would supply the missing words in a whisper to himself.

"RUC own the whole goddam street. Fucking Protestant fucking enclave."

Then the car would be through the town, the two-storey houses giving way again to the clustered cottages of School Terrace.

"How soon will we see the spires?" he would ask, knowing the answer, but wanting to match his recall of his father's words with what he would now say. It was something he did when his father told him a story or said a poem out loud; check that nothing had changed.

"You won't see the spires now until we reach

Ballymacnab," his father would say. "But as soon as we're through the Black Banks, you'll see Keady and most of the rest of Armagh."

Before he was ten he knew that Altnamakin, on the outside of Newtownhamilton, was 100% Protestant. As was Blaney Hill.

"Look up at the window ledges on the second floor," his father would order him.

"See?"

The first time he saw them, he was frightened, because he thought they were guns poking out.

"Bloody flagpole holders," his father said with contempt. "For flying Union Jacks."

Had his father been a spitting man, he'd have spat then. The boy had asked what Catholics put in the front of their houses and the father was instantly impatient. Harps – maybe. It didn't matter. They just *didn't* put Union Jacks.

"Triumphalist bastards and throwbacks," his father would say and get into good humour again.

The conflict between them later on was not congruent with the words he remembered. His father, in thwarted effort to restrain the son from action, denied their meaning. You said things like that, but the only reason was that it got things out of your system.

The silent man had begun his silence, then, opting for a grim-faced uncommunicativeness which went deeper and wider than adolescent disregard for parents. He began to listen and analyse what he was told. He began to listen to conversations on all sides of him.

Almost as a gesture towards an old, unneeded discipline, he now tuned in to the conversations at tables near him.

"I'm sure he said 343, but we couldn't get in."

"We liked the B Plan better, but they were all out by that point."

"You know I never got the updated carpet? I got the old model home carpet and it is so cheap and chintzy and it shows every little speck . . . "

The silent man mentally closed down that conversation and listened to his left.

"My daughter has this hassle with 911, you know? I tell you, they want to know where your exits and your entrances are, and you have to have steel rods that go clear from the ground up, so that the building can withstand one hunnert and sixty mile an hour winds, and it's gonna cost her $350 just to have the plans drawn up to satisfy 911, can you believe it?"

The silent man had thought that 911 was the emergency number you rang if your house was on fire. However, he knew that a reference or explanation would present itself to him in the next few days. They had taught him that, too.

You don't need to know everything now. Not now this minute. Don't be caught askin' questions. Questions make people uneasy. Just pay attention. You'll get the answer.

For a time his silence was integral to his task, his calling. He was a mute monk, ordained to a brotherhood, committed to a code that was tattooed on him through the sharp needle of race memory. Later he lost his faith. Put the code, the tradition, the adrenalin-rushing secret journeys to one side, and walked away. It was a myth that you had to run, that they wouldn't let you go. If you kept your mouth shut and they knew you kept your mouth shut, they left you alone.

Strangely the country music in this place reminded him of those times. The slow one playing now. Ketchum. *Trail of Tears*. About war and defeat, poverty and dispossession and despair. Among the Seminoles or the Sioux.

The song cried to a halt, and the tutor announced "a

real fast line-dance that the experienced dancers here always love. *Guacamole!*"

Shrieks of delight came from around the silent man and dancers came running to get in line on the floor.

"Now for any of our dancers who may not be quite so familiar with this one, how it goes is this way. The gentlemen line up in a circle on the inside, and the ladies line up in a circle on the outside. When we get to the chorus each time, the gentleman dances with the lady opposite to him, then at the end of the chorus, the ladies' circle moves forward, and the gentlemen's circle moves backward. Y'all clear on that?"

Nods came towards him, made impatient by the desire to get on with the dance. The music started and the circles started to move. This, thought the silent man, would be the dance he would have enjoyed. It reminded him of céilí dancing at home and it was completely impersonal. The Eyes-man was spinning the Banker's wife at the moment, while the Banker was turning the Grandmother. No coy glances or shy smiles: it was as functional a dancing as a set of *The Walls of Limerick*. At the end, winded, all of the dancers separated back out into individuals.

The tutor was now setting up the last dance, starting, as he always did, with a count of: "Five, six, *seven*, eight – "

The silent man left an average tip and walked to the door, meeting no eyes as he examined something in his hand. The next record was already playing.

"Livin' in a back street . . . forty-seven dead beats"

The warmth settled around him as the door swung to behind him. His sneakered feet made no sound on the drying tarmac. The car groaned heavily before the engine caught, as it always did. He sat for a moment, letting it turn over, and then slipped it into gear. In the rear-view mirror, as he turned the big car, he could see the Widow coming out, accompanied by a man. The silent man passed the couple, driving slowly. The Widow's hands were on her hips. Through the open window, he could hear her crisp parting words.

"I really don't need this – shit."

He made sure not to glance in their direction. She began to walk, as casually briskly as she danced, to her car. Her figure became smaller and smaller in his rear-view mirror, finally eaten up by her car and the darkness. She would look out for him the following week and he would not be there, because once someone looks out for you, they begin to own a small part of you.

It was cooler now, and he was about to roll up the windows. But a sheriff's car pulled alongside, so he left them open. That way, they could see how ordinary and alone he was.

Barter in Stephen's Green

Fran must be getting sophisticated, I thought as I pulled food out of the white plastic bag and began to organize it on the grass. Little phrases on the phone were the reminder of her three months in London.

"Grab a bite of lunch," for one thing.

Fran and I belonged to families who had breakfast, dinner and tea and never talked about lunch, grabbed or otherwise. The change was expected, though. Fran's was the sort of personality which accommodated itself instantly, unconsciously to its surroundings, so that after five minutes with you, she picked up some of your speech habits. London had neatened up her soft aspirate speech, pinking it with glottal stops.

I had tried to match the new sophistication with the picnic, basing it on half-remembered meals in novels, where characters were always going off to the country with hunks of Brie, loaves of French bread, bottles of wine and some fruit. I was not practised at it. Any picnics I'd ever been on up to then had featured sandwiches in the waxy paper the sliced pan came in, tea slightly tarry from a flask, apples and potato crisps. So I had been hesitant in the delicatessen off Grafton Street.

"Could I have a half-pound of Brie?" I had asked, petrified that it would be sold by the slice and I would look a fool.

Then into the fruit shop for grapes, covered in soft bloom like a breathed-on mirror. I put them out carefully on the grass, nestling in their tissue paper. Grapes at home never looked like these. My mother held that fruit should be washed and polished, even grapes. When guests came, there would be a Waterford Glass bowl on the sideboard with greasily shined apples and pears and two bananas on top.

Two expensive shoes squashed the grass beside the grapes.

"Isn't that just beautiful?" she said. Then we were hugging and telling each other we had lost weight – a lying comfortable ritual – and smiling at each other foolishly.

"Listen," I said. "I'm delighted."

She hugged me again, feathery wisps of her pale hair threading themselves inside my mouth.

"The two of us," she said. "At the same time. Unbelievable, isn't it?"

We threw down jackets and sat on them, and I shoved a styrofoam mug of coffee at her. She poked the plastic lid off and sucked the drops from it before putting it down like a coaster on a dinner table. Awkward, I said we must serve ourselves before we talked. The cheese was already going flat – yellow flanks swelled out from under the crust, and I thought perhaps it was bad.

She broke a chunk of the French roll and took some of it, jabbing it onto the bread with a crudely elegant forefinger.

"Beautiful," she said unclearly, little crumbs flying away from her mouth. "I love it when it's like old socks."

I prodded a hole in the skin of an orange.

"You start."

"No, you."

"O for God's sake," she said, laughing, "We're like two oul' wans on a bus fighting over who'll pay."

"Well you start then," I said doggedly.

"How much did I tell you on the phone?"

"Nothing," I said. "Nothing except that it happened."

She pushed hair from around her neck and chin with the back of a cheesy hand.

"OK then. Let's get the facts first. He's a pianist, fifty, divorced, Hungarian. And I love him to hell and back."

"Do you?"

"Yes." Very seriously this time. "I can't tell you how much."

"Does he love you back?"

She nodded firmly and went on eating. Both of us were conscious of anti-climax and wondered why.

"Now you."

The surging liquid feeling in the stomach. I had only to hear his name unexpectedly and there it was, just as in romantic novels they talk of your heart turning over, except due south a foot or so.

"If you laugh I'll kill you," I said. "He's a Christian Brother."

She laughed, and I laughed too, unoffended.

"Jasus," she said on an indrawn breath, "Ingrown Virginity and Co didn't do so well, did they?"

"Who was it called us that?"

"Jim Nelson."

"God, I'd forgotten that. Although how I could . . . he was the one that asked me if I was Saving It for the Man I would Marry."

We smiled, stings taken out of past misery by the present glow.

"I'll tell you one thing about the last couple of years," she said. "I'm dead tired of having men respect me, meaning that they use me as an ever-open ear for their confidences about their fraught relationships with some other dame."

She swallowed with difficulty, and I wondered why I had not brought butter for the bread.

"It was all the same until Ferenc – me being the total friend. The supporter of drunks, the intellectual companion. The good listener."

She beat effectively at a wasp, connecting with an audible thwock so that it fell among the clover, stunned.

"The gobshite. Not going to bed with anyone, but not hurting feelings. And all the time I'm doing the 'take your hand off my leg, I'm a Catholic' bit, some other Chrissie is lying in wait with a sign on saying 'This way in, lads'."

I remembered the party. Fran and Michael Hooper had talked, hands clasped in her lap, their hair touching, for hours. They drank from the same wineglass, and occasionally smiled in a short-sighted way at people who passed and greeted. Eventually there were withdrawn hands and long sullen silences and quite quickly Michael had gone.

"Do you remember that party in Sandymount?" I asked hesitantly.

"Michael and Sandra?" she said instantly. "Will I ever forget it."

I remembered her frantic tears when Sandra, drunk and cruelly exhibitionist had come back into the house, sand-covered, frozen, wearing Michael's anorak.

"You weren't a big help," Fran said. "Do you remember what you said to console me?"

Never mind, I had said. You know Michael, I had said. Michael's not one to put all his eggs in one basket, I had said, infelicitously. And she had laughed and cried in great gusts.

With no warning, music came from the bandstand. Little girls were singing in regimented harmony. Sweet clockwork music box. A priest bent towards them with a conductor's wand, pulling it back from their avid faces as if he was fishing the notes out of them.

"I've slept with Ferenc," Fran said tranquilly. I blushed fiercely. The children were singing 'Westering Home'. My mind, like a kicked clock, began to tick out the Irish words to the tune, learned in school. I looked at the mess of our lunch.

"Have you slept with – hey, what's his name?"

"David. No. Not that – no."

"Well, I must tell you," she said. "The first time with Ferenc, I made a total arsehole of it. Everything was just right, you know?" I nodded dumbly. "And he undressed me and it wasn't a bit awkward or embarrassing – it was like I had learned it a long time ago and it was just coming back to me. I remember for a split second wondering if my bra straps were grey, and then not thinking about it any more. Sort of at the same time, he undressed. Have you ever seen a man naked?"

I shook my head. The beach obviously didn't count. I did remember how the boy three doors down had once, out playing, produced this limp little finger from his shorts to pee in a hedge. The memory came faintly, still reviving my five-year-old's irritation at the interruption in the game.

The choir changed to 'Kitty of Coleraine'. They sounded accurate and bodiless, like a flute.

"Well, I have no brothers, so I'd never seen one, either," Fran said. "I always thought it had rings around it."

"Like a rattlesnake?"

"Exactly. And I said 'Why doesn't yours have rings – is

that circumcision?' and he laughed so much he couldn't do anything at all. That's the great thing about an older man," she said sagely. "He's been and gone and done it before."

We sat and thought about young men who hadn't.

"I mean, do you remember what's-his-name with the quick hand up your skirt going upstairs? Your man with the red moustache?"

I nodded. He had never put his hand up my skirt.

"If getting old means no more of that, God, I'm glad."

We talked about our families and how they would react, serenely inoculated against their furies and concerns. She spat grape pips into a little section of tissue paper.

"Thup" went the spits. "Has he nice hands?"

I described his hands, fighting the feeling that I was lined up in chorus with ten million other women. I was the first. The only one.

"Has Ferenc got an accent?"

Your turn now. Like the grapes. Six left, so four for you. No, no, I'm the hostess.

"He has, but it's the way he puts words together that's so funny. He says things like 'I think maybe perhaps' and when a job is difficult, he'll say 'that's one heavy chestnut'. He's mad about sweet things – he'd eat jam out of a jar with a spoon."

I presented my swop.

"My David – " (trying out the phrase) "My David butters Marietta biscuits and jams them together so worms come out the holes."

Simultaneously, we realised that we should stop talking. We stood and clapped the singers. We gathered and stowed our rubbish. Then walked towards the small Arc de Triomphe on the corner in silence. I tried to think of a way to let her know I understood the height and depth of it, and knew that she understood too, but I was headachy from sun and too much to eat and my face was clenched from smiling.

At the top of Grafton Street, she hugged me again. I could see the red traffic light through her light hair. When we pulled away from each other, she finished off the hug by giving me a little shake, holding my upper arms.

"Be happy," she said.

WHEEZY WEATHER

It begins with the woman in the dress with the handkerchief-point hem. From six feet away, what we are having looks like a conversation. She must begin all relationships by inflicting a trouncing defeat. No gambit for disengagement suggests itself to me, other than the crudity of "have it your own way then".

Sweat blooms across my back and I ask a waiter to open a window. A quick glance from him. Knowing contempt? Resentment? Perhaps waiters do not open windows. Is there someone lower in the hierarchy? The woman gazes at me, her lower teeth showing. Her face is shockingly mobile under the ageing skin.

"You were saying?" I suggest.

It is wrong. She had been awaiting a riposte, not a prompt. The face debates in its folds as to whether she should persevere or abandon me.

Perseverance wins. She goes back over the last point, her voice coming to me on waves of pulse-timed brain static. I pull my shoulders down and breathe to a count, trying to hold each inhalation for seven beats.

At beat three, the breath hisses away like a punctured tyre. There are small puddles of sweat where my glasses sit on my cheeks. I wipe them away with my forefinger.

Make-up comes away with the liquid. Gold Alabaster. Curious, that I should remember that, when I cannot remember what this woman says to me from minute to minute.

"I do see your point," I lie, all the words tightly tubed in air. Next tube-full almost ready. Steady. Speak.

"I must ask you to excuse me. Not feeling very well."

I miss the last syllable.

Veywell, it sounds like. She offers a glass of water, sympathy, condemnation of the overheating of modern hotels – the seeds, there, of her next conversational campaign.

She looks for my half-finished glass, and a mental arithmetic look comes into her face. Two? Three?

I gather my unrelinquished coat around me, unbelted. A momentary softening hits her flexible features as she considers that I may be pregnant. The thought rolls across the landscape of her face like a steamroller, flattening all other possibilities.

Hunched to repel boarders, I am going, going. Squares of patterned carpet go pushing away beneath me, and more to come. Then a different pattern. The corridor. The lift stands, pneumatic lips sealed. I hesitate, then go to the stairs and plunge down, leaning heavily on the banister, almost sliding, feet making ritual passes at the steps. At the bottom, doors whirl in a circle, and a quick prayer accompanies me – Dear God, let no over-enthusiastic lout clip me on the ankle in these doors.

A blast of chill air and my sweaty hair tries to lift away from my taut forehead. The car seat is smaller than usual. I am squashed against the wheel. A muscle flicks at the back of each knee.

The process of driving breaks down into its component parts, like a dropped jig-saw, so that I must remind myself like an L-plate novice to look in the mirror and over my shoulder. The car responds skittishly.

I had a friend once who believed machines needed to be wooed and won every day. Full of theories, he was, and evinced no irritation when contradictory facts were produced.

I can remember nothing more about him than that, and it is a verbal formula, not reality. Heavy-headed, I drive and puzzle. Then I remember I have said it in just those words at some time, to someone in some smoky pub.

"I had a friend once who believed machines should . . . "

So it's only an echo. I don't know if it's true at all. But I'm desperate to pursue the line of thought because otherwise the gasping will overwhelm me. I slide the bra straps down off the mounds of my shoulders but the feeling of being pulled down remains.

A steady trickle of perspiration runs between my breasts and my face is swollen. Even as I drive, I am conscious of my own cheeks crowding below and beside my glasses. I am submerging, suffocating in my own flesh.

It is as unnerving to be aware of one's own cheeks as it would be if – what? The comparison slides away from me. The constriction cannot be distracted by bright thoughts, whatever the psychosomatic brigade may say.

"It is all in the mind, dear." How unhelpful. No value except as an epitaph, and even then unfair, because unanswerable.

Slow down. Jesus. Seventy. More. The cops. Quickly I check. Where are they? A faded memory surfaces, of a newspaper diagram showing positions of police-bikes in pursuit and I look in the mirror, seeking the blind spot.

The effort puts me more in thrall to the pull, pull past the block. It's like trying to blow up a balloon clasped halfway down its length by strong hands. Never enough, yet there is the need to let the precious ration go in the hope of more next time.

My chin is locked two inches above the well of my neck and there a laboured, irregular pulse thumps in the hammock of thin skin. If the cops stop me it will be the end. The shock will tip me over. Or the explaining.

Say they think it's a put-on? God, I should have a little bracelet. Or a sign. But the thing to work out now is what to say if. The needle creeps to sixty while I work on my lines.

"Please don't stop me, I'm on my way to – "

Too long. If they stop me all I will be able to say is "Please, Please." I whine it aloud, lying into the self-comfort like a child lies into the adult hand banding the forehead when vomiting. Immediately I am worse, lungs locked in spasm. Blackness rolls up and down at the back of my eyes and my heartbeat is louder than the car engine. Mrs Casey all over again. Mrs Casey at the wedding. The story told by the family in hushed tones.

A most shocking thing, my mother would pronounce. And particularly of Mrs Casey, father would add, inappropriately jovial. Neither of them ever described how she looked as she died beside the wedding cake, her empurpled face in the bride's lap. Agony, and silly as well, like your man upside down in the butt of Malmsey. What the hell *is* Malmsey, anyway? Four miles to go. Six or seven minutes? I won't make it. Never find out what a butt of Malmsey is.

Never see family. A faraway sadness there, but not urgent like the need for breath. I can only remember that they exist, not who they are. Neither faces nor names. The smallest one was with me, in me, the last time this happened. Flipping like a little stranded fish inside, poor thing.

But I would sell them, give them away, betray them, for relief. Jesus, yes. In discussions of torture, I always admit that. Quickly, to get the cowardice exposed. I even tend to bludgeon people, strangers, with this unpleasant titbit of self-knowledge. I hear myself at it, boring on with the ruthlessness I expect of old people.

Two miles more. Speedometer at sixty-three. In the suburbs. There is no justice if they don't catch me. I have stopped even looking to right or left, stopped checking my mirror. Every movement, even a head-swivel, uses up this finite supply of vital nothing. My personality is squeezing out of me as an almond squeezes out of its boiled brown skin. One mile. Slow down. It is too near safety to be caught now. Plan the words. Plan them. Two rings on the doorbell or one?

One, if he's there. A wash of terror thrown over my head, spilling over forehead and back. He must be there. Oh, Dear God, he must be there, he must be there. Weirdly, the words arrange themselves as a song, and the name of the singer pops up. Vicki Carr. You see, Mr Cop? The lady with the purple face knows who sang a song, twenty years ago, but try her on her own child's name right now and she doesn't know it.

Entrance-way. No gate. Never noticed its absence until now. No car either. Fat hot tears collect against the lower rims of my glasses. I pull out of the car, make a feeble gesture towards closing the door (it swings open again) and push the bell. No plans. No words really.

I wait, hanging on the polished doorhandle for want of anything else. He almost pulls me into the hall by opening the door. My lips peel off each other and I crack.

"OK, OK." Not stupid, he. Not dressed either. White towelling dressing-gown over slacks. He pushes me gently into the front room, asks yes/no questions. I force something down the air-tube about lateness and he is impatient. He turns his back on the end of my sentence in order to prepare a syringe.

"Going to give you 10 cc of this, so you'll have to ring your husband and get him to drive you home. OK?"

Problems of managing it confuse my mind.

"OK?" It is a kindly threat.

Yes. Sir. Daddy. Anything.

He is sitting opposite now, very businesslike, talking all the time, in quite a loud voice. My children like his voice, especially if injections are involved. He carries them along on waves of cheery sound, and the discomfort is over before they notice.

Tensing for the pin-prick absorbs the last of the air. My nails turn blue. A chilly calm settles into me while I await my next heartbeat. He draws back the plunger and red blood clouds the clear liquid. Then reverses it, slowly, slowly, and the heartbeat comes, followed by the rinse of colour and the unclenching.

I don't know your name either, little friend, little 10 cc, but keep it up. Lungs soften and expand. It's like being that mop with the label – "Don't Squeeze me when I'm Dry."

Everything becomes spongy, easeful. A kindly residue of pain; X marking the spot. And the baby's name comes back to me. Andrea. I will telephone – Michael. Michael will drive me home. The car will sound odd and lackadaisical going at thirty instead of sixty, and this time it will be just a drive, not a pilgrimage. My ears sing.

"That's right, keep the old head down."

He tells me about golf. For laziness, I slide my head onto his desk, swamped by returning vividness like wearing new spectacles – that illusion that it's possible to see everyone's back teeth. The desk smells of lavender furniture polish and his robe smells of Johnson's Baby Powder. Perhaps with small children in the house, everyone uses the same.

The syringe is empty.

"What's that called?"

"What? Oh. Aminophylline."

Amino-off-illeen. Nice name for a little girl. A better ring to it than Andrea. Bubbling with the excitement of relief, I tell him, gushing, that I had thought this one would be final, the worst one.

He smiles, pulls the needle out below a pressing finger and bends my arm over the tiny wad of cotton.

"I wouldn't worry about it," he says, comfortably. "It's wheezy weather. All my chests have been in to see me. It was just an episode."

He pushes the phone towards me, and I dial, planning calming explanations. Michael's voice is tired, puzzled and words pour out of me.

It is over.

THE SCATTERING OF MRS BLAKE

WHEN THE LIMOUSINE'S HORN SOUNDED WITH ARISTOCRATIC subtlety outside, Thornton hesitated. Take the cup or leave it? It was full, steaming. Leave it, he decided. Thin plastic; the heat would scorch his hand and he'd very likely spill it.

"Bloody hell," he said, and stuffed the rest of the bread into his mouth, tamping it into place with a stiff forefinger. He grabbed his anorak and threw it on with such careless energy that the hood bounced up from the back onto his head.

He was shrugging it off and chewing the dry bread as he ran across the tarmac. The limousine purred gently, like a kettle at simmer point.

"Sorry," he mumbled, spraying crumbs. "Breakfast."

Morrissey waited until the door had closed and then moved the big car forward with ponderous stealth.

"You might at least have worn your collar," he said reproachfully.

"Why? I know I'm a priest. *You* know I'm a priest."

"Yeh, but that wathery-eyed oul' git in the Volkswagen doesn't know you're a priest, does he?"

Thornton glanced over his shoulder. They were being trailed by a VW Beetle, left-hand drive. The figures on its number plate were thin and tall.

"That him?"

Morrissey nodded in a curiously condemning way.

From his anorak pocket Thornton pulled a collapsible Roman collar on elastic with its own hanging bib. He slotted it around his neck and leaned back.

"Why were they here – holidays?"

"Oh, this was going to be *the* vacation," Morrissey's American accent was confidently inaccurate. "Mr Morrissey, my son and I are visiting the old country and we're going to take our time about it. We just plan to travel when we feel like it, so we have our own car, because we're used to it, you know . . . "

Morrissey gave a soundless laugh, a mere shudder of the diaphragm.

"And then th' oul fool goes off to Clonmel and drops dead. Three days after she arrived. In Clonmel. Who the hell goes to Clonmel? Nothing to do, even at the weekend but come out and watch the bloody bacon slicer. And I have to go all the way down there and haul her up here and hold her in me sitting-room for a week until he finally gets her incinerated."

Morrissey sighed deeply. It was the sigh of a man who has mentally moved on from the subject in hand, but will not throw out dirty water, conversationally speaking, until he gets in clean. Thornton, meanwhile, covertly examined the back seat of the car.

"Oh, she's not inside," Morrissey said cheerfully. "Think I'd have her spilling all over me nice clean upholstery? By Jesus, I wouldn't. She's in the boot. And that's what I was going to say to you. She's in a damn nice jug."

"Jug?"

"Jug. Urn. Sort of vase, do you know?"

"So."

"So I want it back. I don't want it scattered after her.

There's a polythene bag inside the jug." He swayed fatly towards Thornton like an inflatable dinghy and dug him in the ribs. "She can be scattered out of the polythene bag, so she can. All right?"

Thornton watched the road. Already he was developing that clenched feeling at the back of the knees, that need to stretch and relax the muscles, which meant that he was physically doing something he was not mentally committed to.

"You can do what you like as far as I'm concerned. I still don't really understand why this guy wants me there. He doesn't want a service, doesn't want prayers read."

"Look, Father." Morrissey was suddenly fixed in his role for the day. He was Mentor to Young Priest. The discomfort of the earlier moments was overcome. It was like a dislocated limb dropping back into its socket.

"Look at it from my point of view," he advised. "His mother goes off to America as a girl and meets his father. As far as I can tell, she never marries him though. Maybe he was married already, you wouldn't know. But anyway she loses her faith, makes a right shit out of the whole religion business."

Out on the open road, the limousine picked up speed with a quiet assurance not unlike a heavy pensioner moving into an old-time waltz. The VW chased it, sounding like a muted motorbike.

"Then she comes over here and bloody dies. In Clonmel. Now naturally he doesn't want graves and Monsignors and Mass cards and celtic crosses, but Jesus, he wants a bit of dignity for the oul' trout's last journey, what? In this country dignity equals having a priest there, even if he does feck all," Morrissey concluded.

Thornton kept his eyes to the front, to avoid car sickness. He never became sick in his own car, but then he was always *driving* his own car. In someone else's car, as a passenger, it was a matter of time before his skin began to tense. Looking ahead, blinkered-horse fashion, tended to help. Dignity. Yes. Presence of priest. He breathed deeply.

"I suppose in the end, it's not a bad function to fulfil," he said aloud. "There's couples now getting married and they never set foot in a church after that until it's time to baptise a baby, and then it's only because of getting the child into a school. Still. Being a witness to auspicious moments is better than nothing."

"Keep your eye out for a likely spot for scattering," Morrissey instructed.

"Well, this looks nice, but there's picnickers."

"Jasus, that won't do. Don't want her getting into their sandwiches."

"Why did you pick this hill anyway?"

"I didn't. She did. Or maybe 'twas your man. What he said to me was that she wanted to be scattered on Slieve Rua because she'd done most of her courting there."

"She's going the right way about making sure nobody else does their courting here," said Thornton, surveying his side of the road.

"Yeh. A roll in the hay is one thing. A roll in someone's dead mother is another. I'll tell you, it wouldn't suit me."

"Well, James, I'm not surprised. You're a bit past that kind of thing."

"No, I mean being a witness at suspicious moments."

Thornton's larynx contracted around a correction but he halted it before it found voice. Of late, he suspected Morrissey of larding his conversation with Malapropisms in order to flesh out a character he was developing for himself: two parts rural yobbo to one part Mafia fixer. It was Thornton's further suspicion that Thornton was working up to something on the lines of a Dáil seat and he was very much afraid that if this proved to be the case, he would find himself dazedly canvassing for Morrissey without quite knowing how it had come about.

"Don't miss any good spots now," Morrissey reminded. "No, it wouldn't suit me at all. I don't like things to just happen. Somebody should be in charge."

"Like you?"

"Like anybody that's a good organiser. Wouldn't this do nicely, now?"

The question was rhetorical courtesy. The limousine was already pulling into one side of a paved viewing area. With ostentatious delicacy, like a man pretending not to hear a phone call in an office occupied only by himself and the recipient of the phone call, the Volkswagen moved to the other side of the viewing point and parked, the lawnmower sound dying sporadically to a halt.

"Wrong petrol, the eejit," Morrissey judged, when the post-ignition had finally quit.

Thornton dragged the zip of his anorak up to his chin, reversed it to show the Roman collar and got out of the limousine. Mr Blake, who was indeed quite strikingly watery-eyed, approached in a sidelong walk which implied willingness to shake hands but an ability to take a rebuff without offence. Thornton took the cold bony hand and murmured condolences. Mr Blake dabbled at his eyes and his nose with an impartial and very large handkerchief. He looked wetly prostrate and uttered a strangled sentence which Thornton deciphered as meaning that he was suffering from hay fever and had no antihistamines.

"Father?" Morrissey called.

The boot of the limousine was open but Morrissey's barrel body blocked the contents from view.

"Here she is," he said to Thornton, when the latter had put enough distance between himself and Blake. He lifted a tightly packed bag from the neck of a Wedgwood-type urn. The bag was closed with an elastic band to which was attached a pink label.

"It's her all right," said Morrissey, reading the label. "Pink for a girl. Hold her a minute."

Thornton took the bag. It was unexpectedly heavy.

"Reverend, I would be most appreciative if you would stand right over here."

Blake had a camera in his hand and was gesturing Thornton towards the edge of the path.

"Oh, God, you do it," Thornton hissed to Morrissey.

"Be your age," Morrissey retorted. "He doesn't want a picture of the undertaker fer Chrissake."

Thornton limply walked to the indicated position, and stood, holding out the bag like a fisherman's catch trying to decide whether to smile or look serious. Serious, he thought, and instantly looked grim. Blake clicked the shutter of the camera and it blew a long raspberry and stuck its tongue out at Thornton. Polaroid, he told himself fiercely, corking the frothy laughter. Polaroid. Snap, tongue out. Will you join him, Mr Morrissey? Thank you. A little closer? Snap, tongue out. Just one more. Snap, tongue out. Blake carefully slid the square snapshots into his wallet.

"Thank you," he said. He did not offer to show them the result of their posing.

"Right, Father, proceed." This from Morrissey who had assumed a major-domo stance by the limousine.

"What do you mean, proceed? I'm not supposed to *do* anything," Thornton hissed.

"You're not going to fight over a woman's remains and her poor son watching her?" Morrissey asked reasonably.

Thornton licked gummy lips. Oh, God, he thought. Please don't let Plus-Robert hear about this. I will be sent to Outer Mongolia. Or worse. He undid the neck of the bag.

"Put your hand in," Morrissey said encouragingly, "and take out a few handfuls."

Thornton sent him a look which steamed and seethed.

Then, with great decision, he moved out to where he could see over the edge of the hill, put a hand under the rounded rump of the polythene bag, held the opening wide with the other, and let fly straight into the wind. Mrs Blake's lightweight remains sailed out of the bag, were snatched by the wind and thrown all over his clerical black. He stood, transfixed by his inability to do anything about this plenteous powdering of alien dandruff.

"Merciful God, imagine not finding out in advance what way the wind was blowing," Morrissey said disgustedly. "You wouldn't spit into the wind, would you?"

Thornton turned sideways on to Blake, his back to Morrissey, and pointed the bag, now containing about half of Mrs Blake, downwind. The ash poured out in a steady stream like an ad for table salt. He had an irrational desire to write his name on the hillside, piped in ashy whiteness. A few grains of ash remained in the corners of the bag, trapped by the collapse of the plastic on itself. He crumpled it in his hand.

"Throw it after her," came Morrisey's instruction, and reduced to feckless obedience, he tossed the bag into the air, his natural athleticism giving the gesture an unintentionally sporting flavour. The wind took it and lifted it over their heads, the little pockets of cornered ash clearly visible and then dropped it a yard from their feet.

Thornton turned his back on the bag as one closes the front door behind a guest who has overstayed his welcome. He grasped Mr Blake's cold hand. It felt like a bunch of round pencils.

"Reverend, you have made this a momentous occasion," Blake said, his eyes still wet. "Mr Morrissey."

Thornton waited for him to finish and then realised that the name had been in the nature of a verbal heel-click. Mr Blake strode off towards the edge of the roadway, passing the polythene bag without looking at it. It rolled over and followed him, rotating on its air-filled edges and then wrapped itself around a rock. Morrissey moved with dignified speed, like a swan swimming fast, towards the limousine.

"Your door's open."

The undertaker spoke across the roof of the car.

"All we need now," he said, as he opened the door on his side, "is for him to sell those pictures to the *Advertiser.*"

The big car moved down the hill almost silently. Within it, spurts of conversation.

"Sweet . . . I'm still covered in ash."

"Well, don't brush her off on my upholstery. It's like turf ash, that stuff. Leaves a chalky mark. I don't know why you didn't give yourself a fine good brush-down while you were there."

"It's not exactly the done thing to brush a man's mother off you and he watching, is it? Oh. She's even in the turnups of my trousers."

"Let her stay there till we get home."

There was a silence. Beginning to be car-sick again, Thornton gazed ahead wishing the car had a radio. A great distraction from creeping nausea, a radio. Still, it would be inappropriate in a limousine. Good word that, inappropriate. Very useful in social work. "An inappropriate response." Covers a multitude, like charity. Father leaves mother for blonde temp, mother knocks three-year-old downstairs. Inappropriate.

He pulled the Alice-band clasp of the Roman collar from around his damp neck and stuffed it in his pocket, tried to convince himself that this cooled him down. The movement sent a faint mist of Mrs Blake ash particles into the air and they danced mesmerically before him in the strengthening morning sunlight. There's a biggish flake, he thought. Wonder which – no. *Hic sunt dracones.*

The car drew up alongside the kerb just far enough

from the dip of the road to ensure that its tyres met no small items of garbage.

"Here."

Turning, Thornton found a twenty-pound note, folded longways in Morrissey's hand, being poked in his direction.

"For scattering Mrs Blake," Morrissey said.

"Oh God," Thornton said taking it. "The wages of sin."

"Not wages," Morrissey corrected. "Strictly a once-off."

THE DEPENDANTS

THEY WOKE TO THE SOUND OF SHOOTING IN THE HILLS BEHIND THE villa. Odd, sporadic shooting, more frightening because of its lack of pattern. They lay in silence for a while, listening to the stammering shots, trying to make sense of them.

It had already been a disturbed night, hot, despite the opened netting-covered window and filled with the noises of insects. He had slept heavily, tangling the sheets with sudden movements, exuding a sweat that smelled of herbs. She had lain awake listening to the jangling harness of the mule in the field below the road. Towards dawn, he had moaned and shifted.

"Honey," she said, taking him by the shoulder. It was clammy. Then, louder, "Honey?"

His eyes were quite suddenly wide open with the insulted look of the startled sleeper.

"What?" Testy, as if she was playing pointless games.

"You were dreaming. You were having a bad dream. Well, you were moaning."

For a moment, he looked as if he was doing sums.

"Yes," he said, already turning his shoulder to her. "Thank you. I was."

"What about?" She leaned over his shoulder like a wall.

"What was it about, your nightmare?"

When he answered his voice was fuzzy with returning sleep.

"Playing a game of football. The eejits weren't passing the ball through quick enough."

She laughed softly, comparing it with her dreams, filled as they always seemed to be with monsters, fire, disease, death and destruction.

"You're shaking the bed." Testy again.

She lay against his back, smothering the laughs and smiling and it seemed a moment later when the shots rang out. She checked her watch, 8.13. God, she thought, it's like when you ring 1191 at home and that plastic voice says "At the signal, it will be." "At the end of the world, it will be eight thirteen and twenty seconds . . . "

"What the hell is that?" he said.

"Well, it's not my fault." She answered his tone, not his meaning.

After a moment, she suggested gunfire, and as if in confirmation, there was more of it. Some of it near the sea shore, some higher up behind the cluster of villas. There were several volleys apparently in answer to each other, then inexplicable gaps. Re-loading, she thought, dredging up what knowledge of guns she had gleaned from Westerns. He climbed over her legs to the window and stood peering through the new green mosquito netting he had put up to replace the worn screen. It filtered the world outside like coloured glass, unless you were close enough to peer through each hole individually.

"Jesus," he said, standing so that his toes were sticking up, avoiding contact with the cold of the tiles. "That's what it sounds like, all right."

"What?"

"Gunfire. D'you see the smoke?"

She pulled herself out beside him and stood on an edge

of the sheet. Smoke hung at a level in the middle distance like the way they had drawn mountains at school with a ring of cloud just below the final peak. She asked him what he thought. It was a morning habit of hers, to keep him talking by offering him little questions. It meant she could stay in a cocoon of silence and he grew into good humour as he talked.

"Well, God, I don't know," he said. "It could be anything. They could have invaded Gibraltar or something."

He began to search for clothes, thumping wardrobes closed. He was so vigorous that being in a small room with him reminded her of the sensation of standing behind a car's exhaust pipe when the engine was running. The blast of warm air had the same invading quality and the same kind of warmth.

"Although I don't suppose we'd hear it from here. Bloody Gibraltar's several years away according to Fodor. Unless it's a local thing . . . "

"The peasants are revolting?"

He gave a brisk token smile, already dressed in shorts and a T-shirt, ready for the day.

"What are you going to do?"

"I don't know, I might have a swim before I go in to Nerja to collect the paper."

The depth of her silence reached him.

"God, love, there's no need to be frightened, I mean whoever's doing it isn't going to come and get us. Have you said bugger Franco recently?"

It was a reference to their honeymoon ten years before in the Canaries, when a British trade Unionist on an alcoholic holiday had shouted that slogan with such raucous repetition that most of the people in the hotel had been quite glad when he was arrested. Although all had cooperated in giving him a martyr's welcome two days later when he returned thin and chastened and in the same incongruously yellow shirt he had disappeared in.

"Nobody remembers Franco and anyway I'm not frightened," she said, cross with the lie. "Just will you carry the air-bed down to the pool for me? If you're going, I mean."

By the time they reached the pool, the group they had dubbed the "First Sitters" were already there, a little less dispersed than normally, when each occupied a stretch of grass as circumscribed with towels and umbrellas as if a cable had been thrown around it. Today, they had eased themselves over their own boundaries.

Mr Tattoo, usually seen and nodded to only in the course of a swim around the pool, was – unusually – sitting under the palm tree stirring the unnaturally blue water of the children's pool with the hose used to water the flowers. Her husband nodded to him. It was a nod which discouraged conversation, but for once, Mr Tattoo was in the humour for a chat.

"D'you know what that lot's about then?"

She shook her head.

"We were hoping someone who's been here a bit longer would know."

"Well, I've been over for four weeks, and I 'aven't a clue. I know what it sounds like, but I've been telling the kids all kinds of fairy tales. Problem is I can't do that with Ruth. She's very, you know." He made a fluttering gesture with his stubby hand.

Brian swept the air-bed free of non-existent twigs and took a stance which combined eagerness to be off and willingness to share Mr Tattoo's worries in unequal measure.

"I may find out something in Nerja," he said. "Do you – can I get you anything?"

Instantly, Mr Tattoo began to fiddle with the waterproof

pocket of his swimming trunks.

"Yesterday's *Daily Telegraph*, if they have it," he said, adding apologetically to Anne, "the crossword, you know."

She wondered why he needed to make excuses. He reminded her of an uncle who shamefacedly bought the *News of the World* for years, claiming with gusty bravado that it was best for sport. Brian took the Spanish small change irritably. She could hear him rattling it in his hand as he walked to the little Seat hire-car. For some reason, he never regarded coins as real money, preferring always to deal in notes or cheques. At home, she would find little piles of silver and coppers like worm-droppings in odd places around the house where, pulling out a hanky, he had rid himself of a handful of pennies and fivepenny pieces.

"Well," Mr Tattoo said, worriedly. "I suppose . . . "

"Yes," she said, willing him to go.

After a moment he swung his legs from the children's pool which attached itself to the big pool like a little comma to the tail of a big one and, sliding in to the deeper end, slowly stroked across to where his wife was.

Ruth, thought the girl. I would never have thought her a Ruth. Some hearty British barmaid name like Mabel or Betty or Myrtle. That's one of the problems about staying a month instead of just a fortnight. You get to know the people and they knock hell out of your nice makey-up stories about them. Mr Tattoo'll turn out to be some harmless civil service clerk, she thought, as she watched him pull himself out of the water on the other side. He was stocky and sinewy, and his wife – Ruth – was tall and almost freakishly fat. He treated her as if she were a consumptive five footer, oiling her every day on all sides so that she was a mass of burnished rolls beneath the umbrella.

There were more shots in the distance. Perhaps, Anne

thought, it was going away. And immediately felt guilty. If there are people going to be shot dead I shouldn't care whether they're near people or far people. Her leg was suddenly riven with pain. She leaped up, confused and gasping.

"Oh, Gawd, I'm desperately sorry. The little sod bit you. You can't watch them all the time, can you?"

The baby beamed and slobbered, trying now to reach the gold rings on her beach bag. She reassured the mother, smiling and poking the bag nearer the baby.

"Would it be very dreadful if I left her with you for a few minutes? It's just that I got no sleep last night because of all that shooting . . . "

Anne smiled and agreed and wondered how long a few minutes would be. Was the girl planning to make up her night's sleep?

"My mother says it's a socialist revolution," the girl said, smiling as if this was a pleasant weather forecast. "She thinks they'll come in here and shoot us all like capitalists. I told her that doesn't happen anymore."

"Well, I suppose they must feel we're very privileged," Anne said. "Look at this place."

The man Brian called the Toper, on the flimsy evidence of a whisky glass carried to the pool one evening, spoke suddenly from behind her.

"Do you own one of the villas?"

"No. We're borrowing it from a friend."

He nodded heavily as if this made sense of what she had said.

"I do. Own one. And I worked hard for it. Bloody hard."

Anne blushed and burned with baffled rage. Do you really think you work as hard as that poor old man with the mule going round in the heat of midday ploughing with a thing you'd see in a book about the history of agriculture? A single harrow? Dragging the thing through that dead red clay and shouting the animal on course, all through *siesta* time and then going back to peel potatoes in the hotel at the bridge in Nerja?

You, with your advertising executive's hands and your specially designed-to-be-overheard talk and your silly fart of a wife with her "Swim the way we taught you in the South of France, Darling" to your dreary seven-year-old? Her mind suddenly filled with the bent dusty man in the pale straw hat and the dried-out shoes pulling his way through the awkwardly shaped field. She maintained a curdled silence.

The young mother gave the baby a gentle root with her toe back on to Anne's rug.

"I can't believe they'd be political enough to have a revolution," she said comfortingly. "I mean, they're so primitive, they're still going round with mules."

Nobody commented.

"Back in a few minutes," she added, and walked away quickly, her flip-flops making halfhearted applause on the gravel.

Anne watched the baby, and the baby watched ants. Not for the first time she wondered why babies and their mothers always gravitated to her. She had no idea how to relate to children younger than ten and no interest in learning. Bored, she slid polaroids on and surveyed the hills behind the villas.

Puffs of smoke appeared, strangely out of sync with the sporadic shots. Unexpectedly, there was a burst of shooting much nearer. Around the pool there was consternation.

The woman who never let her children go into the pool without earplugs and who consequently had to yell at them all the time now screamed at them to come out at once. Mr Tattoo helped his heavy wife into a sitting position and talked to her gently, as if he expected her to faint. The baby stared at Anne in total silence, its eyes filling up with tears.

"Ah pet don't cry," she said, trying to hug it.

It stiffened and turned its face away from her. Glancing over it, she could see the mother coming towards the pool, the one figure contradicting the flow of traffic towards the villas.

"I didn't do anything," Anne said defensively.

"Oh, I know," the girl said with a bright empty expression. "It's just the shots. But I think one should be indoors, don't you?"

She spoke with a sureness borne, Anne surmised, of British race memory. Reference – shooting. Action to be taken – move indoors. Roll bandages. Brew beef tea. Anne was conscious of a desire to follow her, to get a wall behind her. But she stayed, mesmerised by the water (calm now after the turbulent children had left it) and wondered how afraid she was. She was, she decided, mouthing her thought to help clear her thinking, she was afraid of the small possibilities but not of the large. Afraid of pain, but not of death, mainly because she didn't believe death was ever going to happen to her. Logically, yes, it had to.

But inside her bone she knew she could never have not existed, and therefore could never in the future cease to exist. So it came down to fear of pain. If she was going to be shot, where would she prefer to be shot? It was a game she constantly played; if she was to hit something in the car, would it be a bus or a bike? If Brian was going to die, would she prefer if it was before her or after her? In the beginning, she had tried to involve him in it too but he had stared and shaken her off.

"What do you *mean*, would I prefer to be blind or deaf?" he had demanded, almost furious with incomprehension. "How the – I mean, what sort of a question. I don't engage in that kind of fruitless speculation."

She had smiled, perversely pleased with his choleric refusal to be drawn.

"And if you do," he had added after a moment's thought, "I'm not surprised you can't sleep at night."

After a while she looked at her watch, frowning the clear sun-spots from behind her eyes. Fear began to slide over her like a cold wet towel. An hour and fifteen minutes. Even if he had to wait for the papers to arrive, he was never longer than forty-five minutes. She sat up clutching her knees to stop her legs shaking. Her mind went into a kind of spasm as it had when the plane was about to take off, all she could think of was a series of unrelated phrases from the Hail Mary. Fruit of the womb, she thought desperately, trying to get to the next bit. Fruit of thy womb. The shots seemed to have halted.

This was more menacing still. Please, Brian, don't be dead. Please. Fruit of thy womb – desperately she went back to the beginning, started through it again, halted, ready to be sick with relief when the characteristic motorbike noise of the little Seat buzzed up from the lower road. She forced herself to gather up the towels and fold them, her hands shaking. Then the airbed, locked to her side by her elbow weighed her down with its bulky lightness. She walked tilted to one side, balancing it. A voice beside her hoarsely spoke in Spanish. She turned, stiff with fear. It was the man with the baggy trousers who hosed the gardens of the settlement, occasionally turning the stream of water on the playing children, causing squeals of delight and horror. He gestured at the pool. She gaped at him.

"Oh," she said. "Oh, nobody there."

He stared. She spoke louder as if that would help cross their language barrier. "They were afraid of the shooting – bang, bang?"

He laughed. "Bang, bang," he agreed, and she wondered whether his happiness was in response to her mimicry of the shooting or whether he was in league with the revolutionaries. She smiled at him dishonestly and made a gesture towards her husband's car.

The smile suddenly faded. He began to twist insulating tape around the hose . . . Brian was beside her still jingling coins.

"I couldn't get your man's *Telegraph*," he said. "They said it doesn't come till later. Should I go and tell him? Where is everybody anyway?"

"I think perhaps they were a little frightened of the shooting," she said, distancing herself from the panic with difficulty.

"Oh, Jesus," he said. "That."

He laughed to himself for a moment. It was something which filled her with hate because of her need to know then and there. She fought down the question and he laughed out the breath.

"All of that's bird-scarers. Electronic bloody bird-scarers. The tomatoes are turning from green to red and apparently that's the time they're most vulnerable. So they turn on those yokes. That's why they don't seem to make any sense . . . "

" . . . if there was a pattern, the bird's'd get used to them."

He laughed and mock-patted her on the back.

"Why don't we make the most of the exodus and have a swim?"

"You do. I'll go and get us something to eat."

He let her in to the villa and ran towards the water. She watched him from the balcony. He was a very bad swimmer, rushing and splashing and breathing in bursts. She could hear him faintly although the sound of the mule-harness from the lower field was louder.

Last Line of Resistance

The old man looked at the small knot of toughs on the corner. He neither slackened nor increased his pace. A slow shuffle, and it stayed a slow shuffle. Anybody watching him would have placed him in the seventy-plus group. They would have been wrong. He was fifty-eight. But nobody was interested enough in him to speculate about his age. He was part of the landscape. He fitted. In a city where brownstone buildings were fewer with every passing demolition crew, his grey clothes built him into the picture as surely as if he had been cemented there. His pace singled him out from the general run of hurrying, tense-footed people. He floated along at the gutter-side of the sidewalk. He was not noticeable as a falling-down abusive drunk would have been. He was just there, a slow counterpoint to the main theme of confusion.

He stopped every now and again, hesitating in front of a garbage can. His progress would have looked meaningless to an outsider. He didn't pick a particular trashcan perversely at random. He had learned to detect at a glance which cans had their lids cracked by vandals. Since the new mayor had been installed all the trashcans had immovable lids designed to keep scavengers, human and canine, out. This hampered none but the law-abiding. The vandals cracked the lids for fun and the scavengers followed.

It was his camp-follower status which saved him from the ever-bubbling aggression of the city toughs, but there were other things too. He was too obviously poor to bother rolling for money. He had realised this long ago, and consciously accentuated his visible poverty. He relied on a long piece of twine to hold together the buttonless halves of his coat in front. More twine replaced conventional bootlaces in his high boots. Some men when they drew back from the confusion of jobs and families and all of the noisy things which leaked into a man's ears, would have simply tied on their boots around the ankle with a couple of circles of rough rope. But he inserted twine into each eyelet and knotted a bold bow in the front each day. That, and the couple of stamping steps he took directly afterwards were other parts of his ritual. The stamping had its origin in the days when he wore thick fresh socks. A crease would be sore if not ironed out by a kick or two when the boots went on. He still did it, even though his socks were now thin and closely moulded to his feet with sweat.

He stopped at another bin, sliding his arm in to the elbow with a speed surprising in one who shuffled so slowly. He worked his way through the garbage. On the left there was a glob of wet matter, probably the remains of an apple. The bin was half full of wrappers from candy, potato-chips and ice creams. On the right was a folded newspaper.

His hand snaked out of the bin, quickly stashed the folded newspaper in the crook of his left arm and returned. This time it went up as far as his shoulder. He groped and fingered his way along the bottom of the metal container quickly collecting loose cigarette butts.

Quick to determine size and firmness, his fingers sorted out and left the cigarette ends likely to leak tobacco before he could use them and the cigar and cheroot butts neither of which he liked. The arm came out of the bin, the butts went in to one deep pocket, and he was shuffling away again. He had learned long ago to time the exercise. You couldn't wait for very long or a strolling patrolman would come up and interfere.

The toughs on the corner were yelling something at a girl who was walking in front of him, gaining speed so that within a few seconds, another body would intervene between them. He could see by the toss of her head that she was embarrassed, and flattered, and a little frightened. Look blank, you silly little fool, he thought. They can smell your fear. They're like dogs. It excites them. At night-time, now, you'd really have a problem, he thought, as she disappeared at speed ahead of him.

He knew himself to be immune to their attention. In the old days he carried a hip-flask. He no longer carried anything except what he scavenged from the garbage cans. They could smell it off you. They could smell when you carried something that they might want. He could have told the security firms that. They thought they were so clever, with their ostentatiously careless and down-at-heel delivery men, carrying wads of pay cheques in beat-up document cases. They never dealt with the guilt smell though. He could often guess at what someone was carrying which caused them to exude the scare scent. Spotty young men with their first borrowed condom burning a hole in their pockets; nervous passion seeking venue and accomplice. Old women carrying a roll of fast-deflating money, their clawing protectiveness of shapeless purses an invitation to the roving bandits of the city.

A red light at the intersection told him to halt, and despite the lack of oncoming traffic, he halted. There are none so law-abiding as those who haven't got a turn of speed. A fat woman bounced up beside him, a dragging department store bag slapping alternately against his and her thighs for a couple of seconds while she got her breath.

"I'll just make it," she muttered, and began to trot across the intersection.

All her loose fatness held together by a tubular coat, she joggled solidly up and down as she went, slowing herself down so much by her rolling motion that she might just as well, he thought, have walked. A car came rapidly from the right, and the woman's joggling motion became more agitated. He could imagine the stupid, undirected smile on her face, half to placate a driver who couldn't see her and who, as long as he avoided her, didn't give a damn if she dropped dead on the other sidewalk, half to ingratiate herself with the uncaring people on the facing pavement.

"Here's silly me," the smile would say. "Be nice to me. I'm harmless."

It was the permanent grin of fat middle-aged head-scarfed women getting aboard buses and trains. It was a hopeless gesture of faith in femininity. Because I'm a woman, it said, I should really be given a seat, or a hand, or a smile, or a pardon. But because I'm a shapeless fallen apart overworked excuse for a woman, I don't really expect anything. I certainly can't demand it.

Hence the smile. It dripped off the edges of their faces when nothing pleasant happened and widened to a desperate grin when someone showed them a moment's half-hearted kindness.

The light turned green and he moved with the crowd, noting in some part of his mind the speed with which he was left behind as the steady stream of pedestrians flowed wide of him and conjoined in front of him again, as if he were a knot in a piece of wood. His hands moved at his sides as he walked, remembering, though his brain was elsewhere, the feeling of the wood. First the axe, then the saw. And then, the best part of all, the plane, slicing into the sides of the plank, shedding little curled tendrils of shaved-off wood like the ringlets children used to wear, and leaving nothing but dust. The wood moving from a rough, unmannerly piece of nature to a milk-smooth textured thing, definitively marked by the hand of man.

That was what he had liked best. Some made gardens, but he had not been one for the self-importance of helping nature along a little. He always felt that nature was somewhere around, laughing at gardeners. What the hell was the point of marking out some tiny quarter acre, and planting seeds to come up like rows of little vainglorious soldiers, or in circles like a pattern around a plate, when all around nature had done the whole thing bigger and better? Leave a garden alone for a few months and it began to move away from you, to quit being something you had affected, and to revert to the general condition, like a convent-bred adolescent hoyden backsliding into marriage in her twenties.

A year or two and you'd never know a man had been there. But a piece of wood, treated and painted by hand; that was different. There was satisfaction in knowing that only another man could comprehensively change it in a short time.

He began to feel cold which surprised him. He was, he told himself, well wrapped up. But then it was winter. And he was slower these days. He could never figure out precisely why he was slower. He didn't find walking more difficult. It was just that his normal pace seemed to have dropped. When he had driven cars, he noticed that when you were talking, or listening to music, or just thinking, your speed dropped to whatever was most comfortable for you. With some people that was fifty miles an hour. With others, thirty. Perhaps, he thought, as you grew older the speed you walked at dropped too. Not that it mattered one way or the other. He had no date to meet, nobody was going to mind what time he came in at.

He turned off the main thoroughfare, and made his way through narrower streets. The street doors here spilled sets of steps from their open mouths. Children stared at him with intense momentary concentration, then ignored him. A couple of black men, their chequered shirts bright against the sombre streets, stood together. Their bright-whited eyes followed him, their heads unmoving.

"You're like those goddam Father Christmases with the rolling eyes in Macy's at Christmas", he thought. "Think your heads'd fall off if you look. Or you think I'd notice and turn nasty. Know what you're thinking too. You're thinking that you're not me, and that's really something."

The children grew grubbier, the dogs more in number, as he walked. A pain between his shoulders reminded him, as so many things did these days, of his childhood.

"Round shoulders." He could still hear his mother's frustrated voice. "Round shoulders."

Chronic, the doctor said.

"Bad enough that I should have to pay good money for Marcy to have braces on her teeth. Now you have to have a shoulder brace. You wouldn't sit up straight. Oh no. You don't care how hard your mother has to slave. Bone selfish that's what ye are."

Even today, he could remember his childhood formula for shutting out the nagging voice. Bloodybitchbloodybitchbloodybitch he would say soundlessly. Once or twice she caught his lips moving but she could never force him to tell her what he had said. He learned early to keep his own counsel. He was badly caught out a couple of times, before he worked his mother out, before he decided that her occasional displays of sentimental affection were too rare, and invariably put him off his guard, so that he was more open to her next mood swing. Once he learned that the sequence was as inevitable as night following day, he simply shut down. On everybody. For a time, quite a long time, nobody realised. Eventually, he weighed up the advantages of tagging along with the majority, even on his terms, and decided to leave. That was forty years before.

He turned and walked up the steps of his own tenement. Ten years ago when he had arrived here with his small case, the janitor had looked at him with amazement. He couldn't figure out why a middle-aged man, neatly dressed and obviously sober, should want to stay in a building which was not only seedy but growing seedier by the day. With the scrupulous concern of the innately curious, the janitor pointed out the disadvantages, chief among them the lack of an elevator, the numbers of black tenants, and the proximity to bowery slumland. The new tenant nodded expressionlessly, and for months the janitor watched him for subtly visible membership of the CIA, the vice squad or a strange mafia group. All that had happened was that the man grew older astonishingly quickly, made no complaints about the plumbing or the heat or the light and only once or twice got noisy when he had a skinful.

The old man set off to climb the three flights of steps. He thought of it as an expedition now and sometimes regretted the lack of windows on the landings. Windows would give him an excuse to pause. As it was, if there was someone else on the steps, he had to keep going, his lungs pumping against his ribcage until he was out of their sight. He always liked to have a nugget of thought to worry on while he climbed. Sometimes his mind was a blank when he began to climb and he would find himself counting. A couple of times, ridiculously, he found himself muttering prayers. His mother would be delighted, he often thought, to feel that the bums-together ritual of the family rosary would now provide him with Hail Marys to pace his faltering upward steps.

A colourful circle. His sister in reds and turquoises. His father in brown. His mother in purples, always purples and always twin-sets. These days, his own clothes were all growing to have the same basic colour. Colours merged with age, while texture grew more defined. His knitted pullover was now a skeletal testament to his sister's busy fingers and brainless activity. He could remember the last time he saw Marcy, her eyes protruding, her hair unnaturally dark over her pale powdery face, those once-braced teeth triumphantly protruding, stained and aggressive. She brought the sweater, and cleaned up his room while he was out walking. For several minutes after he had come back, he couldn't concentrate on what she was saying because of the strangeness of the room.

He had felt like a frostbite victim too suddenly pulled back to warmth and civilisation. The prickling pain was exactly the same. His eyes wandered restlessly over his room, not only trying to locate familiar items, but trying to remember what had been in the blank spaces she had left. A kind of desperation had seized him, as if he was on a TV panel game where the prize for reconstructing exactly in his mind the picture of his room was to have the room back the way it was.

She hugged him, clamping his unresponsive arms to his side, first kissing him on the face with those papery lips, then, nauseated by his breath smell, putting her face in his neck so that her strange coloured hair tickled his nose. She talked at him endlessly. He could have borne that. He had long ago learned to let words flow over him while he listened to the white music of his blood in his mind. But she would finish every other sentence with a question, emphasising it by touching him on the knee or the hand with her ugly, brown-stained old fingers.

He gazed with a kind of fascination at her wedding finger, aglitter with a cheap paste gem. Imagine her still wearing that.

"Keeps me safe," she giggled, when she bought it. "Keeps off the wolves."

Safe from what wolves, he wondered again, and his secretive retrospective laugh drove her into shrieking near-hysteria.

"What're you *laughing* at, for heaven's sakes? What's so funny? I mean, I come up here to this *hell* hole, and I make it nice and homey, and clear out some of the *filth*, and then you *laugh*?"

She went on and on and on until his hands, hands that had shaped wood with such love, twitched with the desire to fasten around her thin-boned throat with its loose folds of skin, pulling tight a sudden sphincter of silence.

He paused for a moment or two outside his own door then turned the handle and went in. Twelve feet by ten. A bed, a washstand, and most of all, a key which was always on the inside rather than the outside of the door. Leave a door locked when you went out and it was an invitation to every junkie in the building to break in, thinking you had something worth stealing.

But at night he locked his door. Not to keep them out, but to make sure that he was in no way involved with them. They could beat each other up, or come home in the DTs, or do anything they pleased, as long as his door was closed against them dragging him in with them.

After he closed his door at night he never left the room again. There was a toilet down the corridor but he used it only in the day-time. At night, he urinated in his own brown-stained hand-basin. He turned the key in the door and used the basin. The plug had long ago disappeared, which was no harm since he rarely if ever used it for the purposes for which it had been designed. The last piece of soap – another present from Marcy – had dried up and cracked across like an old piece of shale, and the cracks had filled up with dirt so that the block of soap looked even older than it was, much as the dirt had drawn a cartoon of age on his own face.

He painstakingly undid the knot of his belt twine, knowing that too rapid an opening meant an additional fraying and a need for a replacement too soon. The ratty carpet was stained with spilled liquid, the more innocent spills like water and tea now blended with bourbon and urine to turn the floor-covering tannin brown. He sat on the bed at its lowest point, the centre of the arc dipping from head to tailboard, almost touching the floor, and took off his boots. He wiggled his feet, his toes stuck together and unmoving because of congealed sweat. Then he carefully laid his coat on top of the bedclothes.

When he got into the bed there was a period of kicking and sorting before the clothes fell into a kind of cocoon around him.

He could remember the women he had brought to this room. Five in all. At this stage they merged together into one female shape, painted, cheaply scented and bringing quick, much-needed satisfaction. Strange how the memory brought back no stir. He couldn't remember in detail any single woman he had been with. Marcy, of course, would blame him for that. In Marcy's unchanging world, there was a right man for a right woman. You were just unlucky if you didn't get to the right place at the right time to catch yours. Or, like her brother, you were an immoral layabout who cared for nobody.

He took off his watch and laid it carefully on the crate beside the bed. It was the one precious thing he had, and even that wasn't so precious. It wasn't of sentimental value.

He just believed in always having one line of resistance left. He could always pawn it.

He looked down at his wrist, a ghost-mark of the watch made him speculate, as he always did, why his wrist was always cleaner under the strap. Did the old leather take up the dirt, or did one simply get dirty only during the day-time when the wrist was protected?

As usual, he thought about a bath. He could remember the smell of clean women, never his own clean smell. A bath always conjured up pink women's flesh, talcum patches on a bathroom floor, and white talcumy footprints across carpet. It also gave him a hot pain across his chest. The last time he had a bath he got so weak that he almost cried out for help. There was a shower on the lower floor but he had never gotten used to them. The noise and the steam and the drumming water-needles against his skin terrified him.

There was no purpose in it. Comfort was in the sameness, the particular warmth of isolation, the luxury of disconnection.

SHOWTIME

SHE LEFT THE BROWN ENVELOPE UNTIL LAST. BIG BROWN ONES with cheap stamps never had much in them. Circular from voluntary organisation, she thought, ripping open the small white ones. When she came back to it what it contained was the magazine. The envelope was unsealed, probably to keep the postage down, but a bit of sellotape had been tacked from the outside flap onto the contents so that when she pulled it out, a scrap of colour tore off. It was a bit of the baby's face. She looked from the torn picture to the reality, half expecting there to be a symbolic answering mark on the skin but there wasn't. He was smooth and clean and smiling. Every time she looked at him he smiled. It made her feel guilty for looking away. The phone rang.

She lifted the handset and could hear the atmosphere in her husband's office. Yes, she was up. Yes, things were fine. Would he like to talk to the baby? She held the receiver to the baby's ear and, almost immediately, his legs began to kick. He squirmed to see his father and she held the receiver closer, pressing it over his ear and against his cheek so she could not hear the baby-talk. He giggled.

"He smiled," she said into the receiver. "And looked for you."

As she talked she propped the receiver in the space between her hunched shoulder and the side of her face and pushed the baby gently off the letters.

"Yes. A note from that bunch in Carlow. Many thanks for your advice and helpful suggestions, they're thinking about them and will be in touch. Card from Therese. Well, what would you think? Drunk on ouzo, having a wonderful time. And the magazine."

He wanted to know all the details from her, even though he would see it a scant three hours later. She told him about the faulty colour on the cover which gave her greenish teeth and the baby a greeny aura around his head.

"Well, you don't want me to read it to you, do you?"

Just give him the general gist, he said. Who's this guy General Gist, she asked and smiled. The baby smiled back and she felt a stirring of contempt. The little hands began to play with the telephone cord.

"Big heading at the top to the effect that yours truly abandoned the career ship to have a baby such a time ago, and our fearless reporter's been finding out how motherhood suits her. Starts with that quote I told you about – scared when he goes asleep that he's dead. And then there's an awful chunk about eh . . . " she tried to paraphrase and gave it up. "You don't expect the vibrant blonde who played Ibsen's liberated Nora with such aplomb to care so much. Or to admit it so openly. But that's one of the unexpected things about her – she's vulnerable. And marriage has given her the courage to say so."

She waited for his laugh, her own ready, and was half pleased to hear him ask her why she didn't like it.

"It's just wrong, that's all. I mean, you can't play Ibsen with aplomb. It's like saying someone drives a tram whimsically."

The baby smiled at her smile, at the laugh at the other end of the line. She had known her husband would laugh a few breaths before she said it. She had tried it out in her mind, and timed it so that the exasperated hesitation and the blurt worked.

"And the 'vibrant'. That's what half-dead political parties describe themselves as when they have an internal fight."

That wasn't so well thought-out.

She read him some more paragraphs and described the photographs, looking at them with perplexity as she turned the pages. Her husband looked odd in them: much thinner than in reality, and peculiarly canny, like a salesman trying to get a car with a broken back axle off his hands while it still went. It seemed strange, because she and the baby looked perfectly normal.

The one they had picked for the final page of the story, just above the column that ended with an extra fat full stop over an ad for an order of nursing nuns, was particularly good of her and the baby. She had him over her head, held firmly around the chest and you could practically hear the gurgling laugh he had given. The photographer was so thrilled that he panicked, did things wrong, and asked her if she thought she could possibly hold it. She had, a line of baby dribble hanging in a long flowing thread between his open mouth and hers. The dribble was curiously cold by the time it reached her tongue. She swallowed it sideways, without losing a smile, and she rolled the baby's ribs gently against the bones of her fingers.

He laughed and laughed and laughed and the effort of holding him there cramped her arms so badly that she found herself thinking the rhymes they had told her to say during labour to stop pushing and it was half a pound of treac-el, and at least they didn't expect you to smile then and half a pound note that's wrong and getting it right will make the rhyme last longer and that's the way the mohoney goes don't come to the end of it because when you get to the end of it your arms break and that's the way and he finished and the baby could be put down. None of that showed in the picture. "Playtime for baby Jame," it said underneath.

"They left the S off his name," she said into the phone. "Half the readers will think they got it wrong the other way and that he's a girl. 'Jane', you know? Well, you wouldn't, really. He's all stuffed into a Babygro and he could be anything. Not that it matters."

She looked at the baby while she talked. It was a he. She would have to stop, mentally, calling it 'IT', or 'The Baby,' and give it its proper pronoun and name. The name was an even bigger stumbling-block. Every time she used it, usually to punish some passerby who had impertinently admired it and assigned to it the wrong gender, the name sounded strange, artificial and a little nasty. It reminded her of plaid waistcoats on poodles sculptured like hedges.

Her husband's voice faded up in her ear. She must concentrate better. Every now and again he caught her not listening and she would say straightforwardly, "I'm sorry, I just didn't hear that *at all*!" The truth, without any justifying reason, always worked up to now. It was like the trick you learned at school if you were an afternoon sleeper and your desk was where the sun came in. You got your chin propped and your head at such an angle that your eyes seemed to be on the book rather than simply closed and if you realised you had been asleep, you didn't start and shake and get red, but quietly listened and sorted out who you were and where. After a time you could afford to look around.

He was asking how many copies of the magazine they had sent.

"Only one, please God it's the extent of the run."

No, she must get more. He would like to have them.

And her mother would, she knew that didn't she, so she must get more and today if possible, in case they were sold out.

"It's unlikely, even given your son's peerless charm, that they'll sell out this issue so fast."

But he refused to laugh and made her promise. At the end she agreed to get some that morning and he promised to pay for them, which annoyed her. Then he had second thoughts. He would buy them himself so that she wouldn't be embarrassed.

"I don't *care*," she said fiercely. "It's like asking for jelly babies – if they're not ashamed to sell them, why should I be ashamed to buy them?"

The baby looked frightened. She put the palm of her hand on his stomach and patted him. He looked at her vacantly. Unnerved, she clucked and the wave of contempt returned as he smiled once again. She took her hand away because the soft, slightly worn towelling was wet.

"Look, I'll have to go. Your son is wet to the armpits."

She changed the baby completely, cupping the small shoulders and knees in her hands competently, although she had proposed to the magazine writer, she recalled, that she was nervous handling this, her first. She wasn't, she thought now as she pushed its head into a fresh vest and mechanically played peekaboo to get it over the fright of the enveloping whiteness. It was like a part she had understudied and taken over, not unexpectedly. But then, *interpreting* the part to a journalist was a role too. As was wifehood. As was motherhood. Reality was the sordid unconfected thing that happened when there was no persona to slip on, no audience to play to.

Halfway through the fastening the baby got bored and cried a bit. She rushed the rest and pulled it up so that it stood for a few seconds on her thighs, supported by her hands, before sinking in to her full hug. It smelled neutral, unlike the boiled milk and talc smell she had always associated with babies. The baby along one side of her, she absently patted his nappied bottom and read the article again. It was not, she decided, too nauseating. True, she had been fed into a slick sausage machine but the end product was at least clean and bright and possibly cheering to others less fortunate. Her mother would certainly like it although she would spot and resent the brevity of the mention given to her degree.

"Jim isn't the only brains around here," her mother would say, "but that kind of magazine always gives orders that wives have to be made out dumber than husbands."

Her mother always got that sort of thing slightly wrong but it would be nice to have the degree noticed.

The baby had fallen asleep over her shoulder. Gently, she shifted so that the fat pad of cheek was against her own and moved her face again and again so that the soft skin whispered in her ear. Without thinking, she squeezed the baby a little, and it gave a trembling sigh in its sleep. Tears rose at the back of her throat and she tried hard to cry, but nothing happened.

CAPTIVA BLUES

"DON'T – EVEN *THINK* ABOUT IT."

It jostled laughter out of him before he turned and saw her.

"Is my yearning that obvious?"

She nodded, her lips pressed together to keep in the amusement.

"I've never been a good bargainer. I suppose that's why. As my mother would say, they see me coming a mile off. What's wrong with it, anyway?"

"How much do you know about software?"

His shoulders rose in a self-dismissive shrug. She considered his ignorance for a moment, kicking a wheeled carry-on out of the path of an urgent procession of departing passengers.

"It's going to be out of date within months, and they haven't designed the architecture right. Plus, it's heavier than it looks."

He upturned his hands in mock helplessness at the sales assistant who beamed past his shoulder at the fair-haired woman who had just denied him a sale.

"So how good are you on free consultancy regarding chocolates?"

"Even better," she said, and he realised she was not joking.

They moved together to the counters where handmade chocolates were ranged for selection. The fair woman briskly outlined the positions on the totem pole of the various brands, surprising him. The brand with which he was familiar came fourth.

"Yeah, I know, you buy them for your wife in the Dublin shop all the time, but that's because you don't know nuthin'," she told him.

He followed instructions and bought a large box of the recommended brand, debating and then rejecting the possibility of buying a second box for his new acquaintance.

"Am I that predictable?" he asked, as they walked the corridor past the VIP lounge on the left. She looked puzzled.

"That you could tell what I'd buy for my wife?"

"If you were as predictable as I had expected you to be," she told him, "you'd have bought me a small box of the same chocolates you bought your wife. But you didn't."

They turned together into a corridor filled with boarding gates and the sound of their shoes was momentarily loud on the hard grey floor as they left the carpeted area. He was filled with a covert glee at being less predictable than she had expected.

"I did actually think about buying you a smaller box," he said sheepishly.

She stopped and laughed. Her laugh took her over in an extraordinary way, shaking her as if a big animal had her by the shoulders. After a moment, she shook her head at the idea and started to walk again.

"Do either of us know where we're going?"

This from him, looking at lines of DC10s and L1011s with their metal noses rammed into the feedbag folds at the front end of each jetway.

"I'm going to Alitalia," she said, looking at him sideways, an eyebrow raised in comment, "but I'm sure you're going to Aer Lingus.

"Usually, yes. This time no. I'm on Alitalia, too."

He didn't need to ask her why she thought he would travel Aer Lingus. No TD was ever safe to choose another country's airline if he or she could choose their own.

But the Aer Lingus flight today had been full.

"I prefer the Alitalia food," she said, as she parked the carry-on beside a row of seating. She knelt on the first chair to read the departure time. "And practising my Italian".

He threw his raincoat over the back of the next seat on the row and sat down on the third. She went into a crouch, still kneeling, on the seat, evidently unkinking tired muscles then slid around the right way and sat.

"I lie. I don't speak Italian."

"That's OK. I don't speak German."

"Oh, I speak German."

"You do?"

"Not really. I know how to say 'I love you', though. Always figure that'll come in handy."

He was checking that he still had the electronic toys he had bought for the children and not paying much attention, when she leaned over his bent head and growled at him, Deitrich-hoarse.

"*Ich liebe dich*."

"What?"

He looked scared. She sat back up .

"Ich liebe dich," she said in a normal voice. "It means 'I love you'."

"*Oh*," he said, relaxing. "You sounded like a dog with distemper."

"I didn't know dogs with distemper got different voices."

"I don't know what dogs with distemper get. I've never had a dog. With or without distemper."

Please, he thought, don't let her say "Oh, you must be a cat person" and define for me the personality differences between dog people and cat people. She seemed distracted for a moment as if she was listening to a Walkman. She caught him watching her and looked slightly guilty.

"I was just thinking how much I hate those people at parties who tell you you're a dog person or a cat person because of your personality. They're nearly as bad as the ones who tell you your star sign. They never get it right but they always behave as though yours was the *only* one they ever got wrong. And they always look at you as if it is your fault, anyway. Like you're only letting on to be a Libra."

A brisk young man was tearing bits off boarding cards and ushering the small number of passengers down the boarding ramp. Robert and the fair woman handed him their tickets and walked together down the slight incline. He noticed that she wheeled her carry-on carelessly so that it hiccupped over joints on the corridor floor.

The steward at the entrance to Business Class put the entire cabin at their disposal in a gesture of theatrical generosity. She slid into a window seat, having efficiently stowed the carry-on overhead, and he sat beside her.

"Unless you'd prefer – ?"

Satirical amusement drove the seriousness from her face.

"Yeah, right," she said, laughing at him. "You'd have no problem at all if I said 'No, Mr O'Hare, I'd really like to be on my own for the journey to Dublin, if you don't mind'."

He grinned at her.

"My wife once got stuck on a transatlantic flight beside an eighteen-carat bore who never shut his beak from the moment the plane took off until it landed. She developed this great fantasy of pulling the toupee off him – it wouldn't have been difficult because it was at a slant to start with – and shoving it straight down his throat."

"Why were you not travelling with her?"

He was taken aback.

"You think we should always travel in convoy for fear we'll be attacked?"

She made a move of semi-apology.

"My wife was on a job. She's a very good photographer. Makes more money than I do."

"More liberal too."

It was a cut as elegant in its timing as the swordplay in an old film.

"True. She's giving me tutorials, though. I may be a slow learner."

"But generous."

"Well, now we know which Sunday paper *you* read."

"I liked that piece," she said, as the steward fandanced a starched miniature tablecloth onto each tray. "Obviously, there was more about you than your wife but I liked the sound of her. She sounded like she knew who she was."

The trays were put down on top of the slightly elevated folds of stiff white cotton and she began to eat with vigorous concentration.

"My wife has a number of great things going for her," he said, watching for – and noting – the slithered sideways glance she gave him of negative expectancy: now I'm going to get the family values bit from this politician. He ate before speaking again.

"She's one of the best in her business. She's physically very strong – not tall, but very strong. Fit. A great organiser. But most of all she's funny. I think that's why I fell for her. She makes me laugh. Always has. Even when I'm in foul humour, she makes me laugh."

She finished the starter, the salad, the entrée and a glass

of wine and was pulling the fluted dish with the pastry towards her.

"Search-and-destroy, is it?"

Puzzled, she followed his gaze and surveyed the empty plates. Her smile had the unselfconscious frankness of a slim woman who can eat and not gain weight.

"Scorched earth, more like."

Over coffee they introduced themselves with a retreat into the formalities they had earlier skipped. She explained her job, which was software engineer with a company of which he had heard.

"Leading-edge, isn't it?"

She nodded.

This time it was he who laughed.

"You missed that bit of evidence," he told her in momentary smugness.

"Bit of evidence . . . ?"

"To prove what a stereotyped gobshite politician I am," he said. "That's a *real* bit of political predictability and you never spotted it. If someone doesn't come absolutely leaping up to you, you ask them how's th'oul' back, and if someone works for a computer firm, you suggest that their particular firm is 'leading edge'."

She smiled at him with the surprised satisfaction he remembered feeling when his youngest child had chosen to roll over for the first time on a day when he had been in charge of him. He wondered would she quote him to her friends.

"What's Bree short for?"

"Nothing. Didn't you ever see *Klute*? Bree Daniels was the character played by Jane Fonda. My mother was into Jane Fonda."

"Bree Daniels was a prostitute."

"Callgirl."

"Prostitute."

"Yeah."

Their trays were taken away and the white linen scooped up. They folded away their tray tables in unexpected unison like synchronised swimmers. The plane banked and announcements were made at them.

"Anyone collecting you?"

Her response was a look of such dense enmity that he was taken aback. He held his hands up at her, palms fending her off in a parody of terror. She shook her head angrily.

"I have my car in the long-term car park."

"What is it?"

"Why?"

He drew a slow breath in through his nose – a lifelong habit of conscious tantrum control.

"Because I am interested in cars. I like cars. I understand cars. I take pleasure in cars. I drive them – although I usually take the train to Dublin and use taxis when the Dáil's in session. I also repair cars. Any further three-mark questions?"

"I'm sorry," she said, straightly. "My car is a red BMW."

The urge for an I-coulda-guessed laugh was enormous in his chest.

"Convertible," she finished, and his laughter roared into her face. After a second she laughed too. The plane landed and they gathered up their belongings.

She was taller than he was and didn't seem to notice. They walked together setting each other's laughter off again like children at the back of a church; the collusion in a half-understood joke funnier than the joke itself.

Neither had luggage. She offered him a lift. He refused without explanation.

"I usually hate the Brussels trip," she said finally. "But this one was good. Thank you."

They did not shake hands. It had not been enough of

an encounter to justify it.

How do I know all of this? I know it because I am the wife. And he told it to me.

When she rang him a fortnight later he knew her voice after the first sentence.

"Hi, Bree," he said casually, interrupting her self-introduction.

"You always that good at identifying voices?

"You always that suspicious?"

It took him a minute to realise that the smothered noise at the other end of the line was laughter. The physical recklessness of her laughter had made him remember it as noisy. But it was almost silent.

"I bet your wife told you you were a bloody eejit not to get a discount sub-notebook from me," she said.

His wife had said almost precisely this to him.

"Find an hour for me to drop into your office and my technology will change your life," Bree added.

"Your technology will change my life?" he asked.

"You don't know how to flirt any more than you know how to buy Belgian chocolates," she told him cheerfully and rang off.

He sat for a while on his own in the office, letting the phones ring unanswered, pleased to be found inadequate as a flirt and intrigued by the revival of the word "flirt". Words he had never come across except in books were becoming current, he noticed. His son, describing a teacher, had talked about her "berating" him, and the word had eddied around in his mind like the half-remembered lines of a limerick.

When she came to Leinster House he collected her from the main lobby, pleased that she had affixed the *Cuairteoir* badge to her lapel expertly. One recent visitor had made a major issue out of the relatively simple clip-on device and complained about breaking her nails. He took her into the Visitors Gallery. A little known Government backbencher was doing his best with a speech obviously written by someone a great deal more pompous than the backbencher. Bree sat in complete silence. No comment. He stood behind her seat, ranking in his head the comments he was used to.

"Gosh, it's much more impressive than it looks on TV."

"Isn't the wood carving lovely."

"Look at how few people there are down there – isn't that disgraceful."

After a few moments, she stood up and he led her towards his office, not pausing to introduce her to any of the people who greeted him by name or glance. When they reached his shared office, Oliver, a TD from the Midlands, was on the phone. He waved his pen-holding hand in an all-encompassing motion denotative of welcome, of apology (for his presence) and of impatience (with the caller.) Robert gestured towards his own desk. He had cleared a space in advance. A sufficient space. Bree shucked the carrying case off her shoulder and unpacked it. When all of the contents were on his desk she re-zipped the bag and put it against the leg of his desk. A weirdly haphazard association formed in his mind.

"Now," she said briskly.

He started.

"Sorry. Miles away."

"Where?"

"Trying to remember the name of the guy who tried to blow up Hitler with the bomb in the briefcase."

"Richtoven," Oliver said, his mouth close to the hand he had cupped over the phone. Robert batted the inaccuracy away like a wasp. Bree waited incuriously.

"Now," she said again. "What do you use a computer for?"

"Writing speeches. Letters. Keeping notes. Compiling – "

"OK? OK? Speeches."

Satisfied that she had silenced him she quickly typed in the beginning of a notional speech, then began a demonstration based on the two paragraphs she had caused to flicker into near-visibility on the small screen.

"Get down here beside me," she told him. "You can't see an LCD screen at that angle."

He dragged over a chair and sat, conscious of Oliver's red-faced pleasure in the tableau. As the demo progressed he could hear Oliver speeding his caller to a conclusion. Dutifully Robert introduced them. Bree looked at Oliver with an expectant air that seemed to wrong-foot him.

"Oh," Bree said, going back to the screen. "I thought you'd make jokes, or something."

Oliver's face got redder as he silently watched the screen. Normally that was what he would have done: tell jokes. Robert, who usually enjoyed Oliver's outdated rakishness, found himself cruelly pleased at his colleague's discomfiture.

"You've made a good decision," Bree told him when he agreed to buy the machine. "It'll do everything your desktop will do but faster and you can take it anywhere. Though they don't let you use them on planes any more, which is a pity."

Oliver's two phones started to ring.

"This is like our service department," she said. "Phones never stopping. We do 99% of our service on the phone. If we can't tell you how to sort out the programme, your machine must have a very unusual problem. In which case we get you to mail it back to us and send you a new one. Simple as that."

She backed out of the door, dialling a circular handwave at Oliver who flailed defeatedly in the wake of his failure to inflict a kiss or two on her. Oliver had briefly been an MEP and thought himself a master of the two-cheek kiss.

"Don't tell me," she said as they walked together, him feeling ungentlemanly because she had refused his offer to carry her shoulder bag. "He makes you laugh, right?"

Robert nodded.

"Come and have a cup of tea in the cafeteria."

She stopped and looked at him. Two people walked between them, heading back towards Robert's office.

"That an ultimatum?"

He smiled at the accuracy of her description of his tone.

"And why the cafeteria? Is it less serious to have a cup of tea with a woman there?"

He nodded.

"Jasus," she said. "OK."

She had scones and poured yogurt on them, tilting the disc of dough to keep the too-runny liquid from pouring down the sides between bites.

"Is that flirting?" he asked. "Eating combinations of things nobody else does in a way that attracts attention to you?"

She sat completely still, a vacuum of attention in the shifting noises of the cafeteria. The blueberry yogurt overflowed one side of the scone and streamed onto the plate.

"I suppose it is," she said.

"Don't waste it on me," he smiled. "I don't know how to dish it out. And I don't want to know how to take it."

"But you'll enjoy people asking you who I was after I've gone."

The truth of it made him nod. The finality of it got them both up and moving.

I know this, too, because he told me. The same day, he told me, wondering at her style. She fancies you, I said, and he looked at me as if I had burped.

It was Oliver who provided a reason for them to be in contact again. Oliver wanted a demonstration of the sub-notebook Robert had bought. He rang her company and they told him on-site demonstrations were never done. They could put him through to their tele-sales department, they said. He said thanks but no thanks, distracted by the prospect of teasing Robert about the blonde software engineer who'd come – untypically – to give him a personal show.

Robert, who knew Oliver's limited capacity to cope with absolute truth, explained in detail how he had met her and why she had chosen to demonstrate the machine.

"I think she felt guilty that she'd stopped me buying the one in Brussels airport. And also she's a big fan of Kits."

"How does she know Kits?"

"Just the paper. Remember the feature about the two of us? She liked the sound of Kits."

Oliver did a "pull the other one" expression.

"Oh, come on, Oliver, you know me too well for that. Freestyle womanising is your department."

I know this, because Oliver told it to me in the presence of his wife. Her smile stayed hanging from her ears like a dropped stitch. She married him knowing him to be faithless and wandering but planning to convert him. She has failed, and he, not knowing about her hopes, dances on them publicly in front of people like me who pretend not to see.

Bree rang Robert back to tell him that she wouldn't demonstrate the machine to Oliver.

"Tell him that you know the machine so well at this stage you could do the demo. If I rang your wife, would she let me buy you dinner?"

The unexpectedness of it floored him.

"You've just plumbed the shallows of my sophistication," he said after a moment.

"Made you pompous, too."

"Why would you want to buy dinner for someone pompous and illiberal?"

"Ah *ba*. So we keep a little scorecard of any crack anybody takes at us, do we?"

"Not normally."

This was not true and he knew it. Not vengeful, he still could not rid his system of the grit of criticism, grinding away at the granules of it over time. Occasionally he transformed a criticism into something worth re-telling as humour. For the most part, however, snideries stayed unintentionally filed in his mind, cross-referenced by source and date.

"My love life is in flitthers," she said. "And I want not to be on my own tonight, and not to have to eat something I've made myself and not to have to tolerate some buck eejit on the make, and I figured Mr Happy Marriage, head of the Faithfulness Corporation, might be a dead safe option."

"All right."

"I'm sorry."

"Don't be."

She named the restaurant and he was late, delayed by a three-line whip. He used the phrase and she ignored it. She was, he thought, purposefully ignorant in areas she had decided were of no relevance to her. And he thought himself subtle in his observation of the corollary: that if she had been trying to interest him, she would have pretended a fascination in his trade. As it was, she sat, surly and un-made-up, pretending no such interest, just waiting for him to help her in some undefined way.

"That's why I was in Brussels. We've set up an office there and the guy who's heading it up is the guy I've been living with for the last seven years. Great job opportunity. Couldn't pass it up. Commute? Nah. Not really. Times move on. People change."

You're very young, he thought. There'll be loads of others.

"And *don't* tell me I'm young and there'll be others. I know there will be others. It isn't even that he was so perfect, you know?"

He didn't, but nodded.

"I just always thought it would be me who'd do the leaving."

"Oh, so we're talking straight resentment here, are we?"

For a moment, he thought she might hit him or weep. Instead, the shaken-by-a-lion laughter took her over. At the end of it she was all business again, summoning a waiter, handing over a credit card and criticising the chicken dish. She offered to give him a lift back to the Dáil.

"A convention-ridden bumpkin like me wouldn't be up to a red BMW," he told her.

"Convertible," she corrected. "By the way tell your wife I saw her stuff in Esquire. Great."

I know this because he had to tell me. And I sickened at the ineluctable punishment presaged by the compliment. A one-syllable Trojan Horse and me the Cassandra with the tripod and the slowly gelling smile.

The after-image of her stayed with him. When you're too close to a flashlight going off, your vitreous humour holds a shadow of the image and floats it down the back of your skull where you can't quite get to it but you can't quite lose it either. He would quote her to others, consciously enjoying the reference to her name. Yet comfortable that the very technical, unemotional content of the quoted comment was not only a *public* protection for him –

against the very notion that he might be attracted to her –
but a *private* protection, which underlined how little they
had in common.

Freed by this notion, he thought a lot about her. He did
not contrast her to his wife, because that would have been
a mental disloyalty, a Jimmy Carter hypothetical betrayal.
He would wonder if her fair hair was real or dyed. (He was
no good at spotting the difference.) He would try to
imagine what kind of boyfriend she should take up with
now. The man in Brussels was evidently not to be pursued.
He would try out in his mind the words she used about the
Brussels guy. She had said she 'lived with him' and
described him as a 'partner'. When constituents and
business lobbyists used the word "partner" it triggered the
after-image and a split-second pleasure safe in its
unconnectedness.

The after-image did not fit the gridded life he led,
regimented to fairness. He once described himself as a man
without instincts, but this was untrue. He was a man
uncomfortable with instincts. In school, in Knockbeg, he
had shown a good eye for composition and colour but had
worked harder at maths and physics out of a family sense
that what was measurable and concrete was necessarily
superior to what was subjective and creative. He was a list-
maker who noted down the left side of the page the PRO
points favouring a particular decision, and down the right
hand side of the same page, the ANTI contra-indicators. He
therefore treated the recurring after-image of the young
woman as tourists treat a resort: nice place to visit but you
couldn't live there.

He did not telephone her. Ever. Men of his type did not
ring unmarried women. Oliver, who gave Robert's repeated
references to Bree an earthy and empathetic significance,
eventually assumed him to be seeing her on the sly. The
fact that Robert wasn't gave him a sense of being much

older than Oliver and wrapped him in a further insulation which allowed him to think about her more frequently.

How do I know this, since he, not knowing the whole of it, never told me? I just know it. That's all.

There was no change in him at work or at home. The decisions had long ago been made about him as a politician. No leadership ambitions. No great ambitions of any kind. Professional. Easy to get along with. But careful – not in the sense of financial meanness; stands his round. Listens more than talks.

He was surprised and pleased by how neatly his public perception matched his interior reality. He was sad for the anxious competent nonentities who saw themselves as party leaders and who came to him ("as a good Party man") ostensibly to seek his advice, in reality for the reassurance of hearing their own assertions made – out loud and unchallenged – in the presence of a third party. The gap between their experience of themselves and the way others experienced them was unsatisfactory to him. But he mistrusted the PR people they employed to polish up their newsletters and introduce them to journalists.

He never went out of his way to talk to journalists but they tended to like him nonetheless. Partly because he was funny. Not *too* funny – dangerous for a politician to own a speedy, brilliant, ever-working wit that creates an audience, a fear and a justification for dismissal. When he thought of a lethal crack he would not utter it except at home to his wife, where it became a kind of gift, smuggled. His mind had become a safety deposit box of unuttered quips.

The journalists accepted his self-presentation as an unambitious professional who made no claims to anything other than ordinariness. He kept secret his own private sense of his absolute uniqueness and neutral insight.

One of the things that intrigued him about Bree was that she was completely outside his world and had no interest in it. As they crossed the plinth outside Leinster House at the end of that first visit, a well-known TD was being interviewed by a TV crew. She looked, but asked no questions, content to let a public image stay a public image. He wondered what she wondered about, or if she ever wondered.

It was the junket that precipitated what didn't happen.

Someone in the hierarchy decided it was time Robert got sent on a trip. No spouses unless deputies were prepared to pay full freight for them.

"Where is it?" Robert asked the secretary who rang him with the good news.

"Captiva Island, Florida," she said, pronouncing it with the emphasis on the first syllable. *Cap*tiva Island. As in 'captivate'.

"Where's *that*?"

"It's on the Gulf Coast," she said as if that explained everything and rang off.

Robert told Oliver who likened Florida to a hanging penis and said the Gulf Coast was on the body side of the penis.

"Who else is going?"

"I never asked."

Oliver looked at him as if he knew this to be a lie.

"You never *asked*? You never asked were any of the women going?"

"Oliver, I don't *care* if any of the women are going. Kits and I can't afford for her to take time off and come with me and so I'm not staying for extra days or anything."

Oliver plunged out the door on a promise of finding out who else was on the trip, broken down by age, sex and political party. Robert rang Bree.

"Don't tell me," she said, recognising his voice. "Your

lust for my body has overwhelmed your defences."

"Does my notebook plug into American power?" he asked, the question so prepared in his mind that he started to ask it before he registered her opening gambit.

"Absolutely."

"Great."

"You lending it or going on a junket?"

"I'm going on a fact-finding visit."

"Where to?"

"Captiva Island."

She immediately corrected his second-hand pronunciation.

"Capt*eeva* Island."

"D'you know it?"

"I was there for three days once. My company ran its annual sales conference in a hotel cutely named the t'Ween Waters Inn, because it sits between two bodies of water. It's beautiful. I mean, wonderful. Take all your notions of Florida and throw them away. High rises and pink plastic pelicans – "

"Flamingoes."

"Right. None of that. Just sort of tropical vegetation and green and sea and white, white sand and shells. They're known as the Seashell Islands."

"I thought it was one island."

"There's a little one tagged on to the first one by a bridge. Sanibel. When are you going?"

He told her and that was the close of the call.

I know this because he told it to me. Because my fears were in suspended animation at the time, I heard it without dread. Particularly because, this time, she hadn't asked after me.

She rang him a week later.

"You want me to buy you dinner on Captiva Island?"

He was distracted by the commerciality of her invitation style. He always invited people to have dinner with him. Never suggested that he buy them the meal.

"God, the enthusiasm," she said, over his pause.

"How?"

"Believe it or not, I have to go to a two-day company course at corporate HQ in Atlanta at the end of the week, and if I went a day or so earlier . . . "

The arrangements were made. Three weeks later, he picked her up from the South West Florida International Airport.

He was wearing shorts and a strip of angry redness down the front of each leg. Her greeting to him was a pointed finger and a silent explosion of laughter. Hands in shorts pockets, he swayed on straightened legs and examined the sunburn.

"Fell asleep, did you?"

She had the same carry-on as she had when he had first met her. It trailed behind her like a well-trained dog. No luggage to pick off the carousel. She was flying back out to Atlanta in the morning. When the darkened glass of the automatic doors parted they were met by blinding sunshine. The humidity steamed up her sunglasses and she stopped to clean them on her cotton skirt. She was in fawns and beiges that gave themselves without identity to the sunglare.

He pointed to his hired car but directed her the long way around, rather than cutting across sodden grass.

"People don't cut across it even when it hasn't rained," he said, indicating the lack of foot-beaten paths. "It's only in Ireland that people like to walk as the crow flies."

The car was not a convertible. The girl at Alamo had told him they could upgrade him to a Le Baron convertible for ten dollars extra per day but he had refused. Sixty dollars could be better spent on something decent for Kits or one of the children. Now he made sure the air-conditioning was working. Bree watched the signs.

"You going to do that?"

A poster for parasailing showed a man hanging below a great red parachute perhaps fifty feet in the air being powered along by a speedboat.

"I would never do something like that," he said, slightly stressing the 'I' in self-parody. Meaning other daft eejits would get up there and trust the lad at the wheel of the boat, but me . . . ?

"Why do you always talk about yourself like a project that's finished?"

He thought about that as he turned from Gladiolus onto Summerlin.

"I suppose I'm realistic about myself. I was never a great man for the solo run."

He pushed the car's cruise control button, and took his foot off the accelerator. The car moved to a steady 55 miles an hour and stayed there.

"I'm a Gaelic football man, did I tell you that?"

She shook her head so that the straight unyellowed fair of her hair moved softly.

"I was always a great team player. Not out of strength – it just fit with me. I had no really outstanding skill. There was a Donegal footballer years back and they actually called him Solo Run. Solo Run McLoone. Because every now and again he'd just take off – "

His hand, straight as a gun, pointed ahead of them down the road at an imaginary goal-mouth.

" – and you couldn't fight with it because he was just so good. So fast. Jesus, he was a joy to watch. But I was best in a team."

"That's not what I meant."

"Oh?"

"You're always . . . I don't know. Talking as if you needed to kind of sign off on the job. As if you didn't mind other people changing, but you were – fixed."

This seemed to him to be so sensible that he was puzzled.

"Nobody's fixed," she said after a minute.

"Well circumstances change all the time," he said trying to be helpful.

"Yeah, but you don't protect yourself against circumstances by declaring yourself a protected building."

Her own use of metaphor – rare, he realised – seemed to amuse her and she laughed in a way that did not seek his involvement.

"Well, how do you?"

"How do you what?"

"Protect yourself against circumstances?"

"Why would you want to?"

He was searching for three dollars for the toll booth.

"I'm told that in winter the queue for this thing is miles long because that's the high season," he said, slowing behind a Pontiac with a roof rack and PADI divers stickers. The transaction was quick. Their conversation was swept to nothing by the beauty of the great curving sweep of the two-bridged causeway ahead of them, its slow arching rises swooped to ground level to touch on sanded islands in the water.

It was like a freehand brush-sketch; sure, yet delicate. Pelicans hovered at the edges of the bridges and people, their white-shirted backs blink-bright in the sunshine, fished in a desultory way. The rubber dividers between the road sections thrummed under the wheels.

She sucked in a breath of air and expelled it slowly like a purgation of all previous existence. Said nothing. Looked at him and shook her head slightly, as if to acknowledge that any comment would be inadequate to the beauty of the place. Looked back at the vivid blue of the sea cut into trails by a Boston Whaler heading for North Captiva.

As the car moved onto the mainland, he spoke. "Bree."

She laughed. He looked at her, baffled.

"You do that on the phone a lot," she explained. "Sort of turn it into a statement. With a full stop after it. 'Bree.'" she mimicked.

He was as embarrassed as if she had flattered him.

"Anyway, go on," she said, imitating the opening of his sentence again and gesturing him to follow; "'Bree'."

"I'm going to have to call you Marmaduke," he complained, turning onto the main road through the island. The tall trees met overhead, chopping up the powerful, all pervasive sunshine into dappled decisive bursts.

"What I was going to say was that I have booked a room for you, because of you over-nighting."

"Presumably it's about a two mile walk from your room?"

"Well, the rooms are sort of chalets as you know, and what I've done is get you one on the Gulf side."

"And you're on the Marina side, right?"

There was a mix of certainty and amusement in the voice.

"Yes."

"Well, that protects all of our reputations," she said.

Anything he thought of saying sounded self-serving. He could think of no facetiousness to take the lumpen pomposity out of it.

When they hit the featureless seven-mile stretch where the road was bordered by mellaleukas and a cycle path, she started to talk about the sales conference. It had been good. In the next two days she would be meeting the International directors and they would discuss with her what should be her next assignment.

"What does that mean?"

"We go from project to project. I'm coming to the end of one of them."

"How are you regarded?"

"Oh, very well," she said, as if this was inevitable. She seemed surprised by the question. "I'm very good at what I do, you know."

"I never doubted it."

She pushed her thin wrists against the red velvet of the dashboard cover, bracing her back against the straight extended arms. He wondered if she had a bad back but felt if he asked her about it she would take it as a seeking for compensatory weakness to set against her professional performance.

"Be overseas, probably."

"You don't get choices?"

"If I want another ten thousand, I go overseas."

"What do you get paid at the moment?"

"'Bout seventy."

She dropped the long slender hands back into the crumpled fawn cotton at her lap and looked waif-like. He wondered if it was deliberate.

At the small bridge joining the two islands she tried to see out of both sides of the car, like a child on a plane for the first time, convinced that staying with one window would mean missing something wonderful through the other window.

He slowed the car when the beach came into view.

"Want to show that to you," he said. "That's why I'm here. It's a recycled beach."

The car turned to the right and they were in the sandy grounds of the hotel. After check-in he left her to her cottage and told her he'd see her at 8.30. He had a meeting first with the rest of the Oireachtas delegation.

"Be as late as you want," she said.

"Not unless you want to eat fast food," he said. "They

close down very early here. We're booked at 9 in the Nutmeg House and that's as late as they'll seat us."

She circle-waved him away and he went to his meeting trying to remember who the wave reminded him of. His view of her was very referential, he reflected. He noticed how things reminded him of her or how she reminded him of other things.

When he picked her up that evening, he made her go back for a jacket.

"For God's sake," she said, as she settled into the car and threw the jacket on the back seat. "It's like an oven out here."

"But we won't be out here," he reminded her. "Air-conditioning can be very cold."

The Nutmeg House had hand-written menus, a limited listing of superb dishes and a trio of young women playing chamber music. The evening passed in quietness, in drifting conversation and in the harsh sweetness of medieval music.

He worked out the schedule for the following morning as they drove back to the hotel. The flight was at seven-thirty. That meant checking in around about six-thirty.

"Not so early," she commented, "s'only a domestic flight."

"OK, then six-forty-five. From the islands, the airport's about forty-five minutes. So we'd need to be up around six."

"What I'd really like to do is get up earlier than that and walk this recycled beach."

"So why don't I wake you at five-thirty?"

"I could do it unilaterally."

"And miss my illustrated lecture? No. I'll wake you at five-thirty."

He knocked on the door of her cottage at five-thirty the following morning, clutching a carton of orange juice and two Danish pastries wrapped in wax paper. He had warmed them in the microwave in his own cottage. They walked across the road to the beach, Robert surprised to find his pocket torch unnecessary. Luminous pallor ran along the line where beach met sea. The soft sibilance of their feet in the coarse pale sand was punctuated by occasional animal or bird cries.

He told her about the sweeping away of the beach in a hurricane. One day it was there, two hundred feet from road to the water's edge. The next day it was gone, leaving a shallow cliff which fell away directly into the sea beside the road. Every incoming wave eroded the cliff further, endangering the road. So they brought a great machine like an oil rig and parked it out in the bay. It sucked up sand from the deep and channelled it through great pipelines. The sand came out at the end of the pipelines like minced meat out of a grinder, gradually building a new beach where the old one had been. With the deepwater wet sand had come shells nobody had seen before. Sawgrass and other vegetation had been planted at intervals to hold the new sand in place. There was a possibility that the technology might be used to rescue eroding beaches in Ireland but it was expensive. Very expensive.

"And synthetic," she said.

"Not synthetic. The turtles came back and nested. Unusual way to create a beach, maybe, but beautiful. Isn't it?"

Tiny white birds walked prissily along the edge of the tide, scurrying to avoid the incoming waves. The dawn was coming fast but still pale. The two of them munched pastries and swopped a juice package between them. When it was finished, he noticed a trash-container and diverted from their path to stuff the package into it.

"A place for everything and everything in its place," she

whispered, making arm gestures like someone conducting a tune.

"Shh. Don't be jeering at me. I'm too easy a target," he said, not whispering although the quiet made him want to. Her acceptance of the frame of his self-portrait made him feel more confident within it. Confident enough to reach out and stroke her arm with the back of his hand – an unlikely intimacy that turned her towards him like a wind-caught kite and brought them into an embrace of ferocious knowingness. He could not breathe past the need of her and willingness of her.

Out of nowhere came a fuming thunder of noise. From behind the back-barrier of beach trees hurled a huge black silvered machine. They ran from it before they could register what it was; a World War II DC3, so near the ground they rushed in a crouching panic along its flight path, frenzied beyond logic by the attack it was making on them. They ran separately, the tornado of noise rubbling them to abject terror, the closeness of it blocking out the paling sky. Then it was past them, but not finished with them. It bombed them, vomiting out two great rolling barrelling expanding falling trails. They tried to get out of the way of the spreading twinned cloud, but it boiled over them in cold – ice cold – black droplets stinking of gasoline, sticking like inert parasites to their faces, their arms, drip-spreading into the cleanness of their clothes.

The sound was suddenly a distant reminiscent growl. Robert's thoughts came back to him like an echo: mosquitoes. They were spraying against mosquitoes. In the early morning before people were up. Because it was the rainy season. Mosquitoes.

He looked towards her, where she stood, splay-legged, holding out her hands from her body as if to touch herself would give her an electric shock. He looked for a clue: laugh or be serious.

She turned to face him, vile with anger.

"You stupid bastard," she said, with ringing clarity and a slowness on the second word that made it hiss at him. "You *stupid* bastard."

She passed him, running. Running now with purpose. Running badly, he thought. Running like women run who aren't athletic. Lightly, but all angles and awkwardness. She ran in the monotone brightness of the dawn until she was opposite the cottage and disappeared into it. Once he was no longer visible to her, he, too, began to run with athlete's efficiency until he reached his own marina-side cottage where he showered (using detergent from the kitchen, rather than shampoo) and changed into crumpled Docker trousers and a T-shirt.

At six, he was outside her cottage. He did not knock. She came out within a moment, locked the building and sat into the car, putting the keys in the open dish space between them. He drove in silence. She never spoke. At the airport, she took her carry-on and in a single movement that was more a twitch than a gesture indicated that he was to drive away. He did.

And that was the end of it. How do I know this? Because she told the one woman she trusted and that woman told another woman and it sought its home as water seeks its own level. Its home is with me. It is an unsatisfactory secret because he cannot talk to me of it and he cannot learn from it. His sums of himself no longer add up, because he knows them now to be sums of circumstance without value. Everyone needs a great sin to have retreated from and he doesn't even have that. He brought home his stained clothes and told me about the plane. As a lone experience. I never expected to get them clean, and I never expected him to wear them again. But I did. And he did. Later in the year I changed my car. Although I chose the same Honda Civic model, I moved away from red. They had a blue, they told me. Metallic sort of electric blue. I looked at it and said yes. When I read the manual I found it had a name, that blue. Captiva Blue. Somebody may mention it to him at some time, but it's doubtful. He will not find the manual: he is not a man to read car manuals. And if someone mentions it to him, he will not assume I knew.